OVERDRIVE

Lawanda,

Enjoy "Overdrive!"

Carmen K. Glenn

June 2011

A Fiction Novel

By

Carmen K. Glenn

Cover image by fotosearch.com at www.fotosearch.com

First published by Dog Ear Publishing
4010 W. 86th Street, Ste H
Indianapolis, IN 46268
www.dogearpublishing.net

ISBN: 1-59858-153-8
Library of Congress Control Number: 2006925735

This book is printed on acid-free paper.
This book is a work of Fiction. Places, events, and situations in this book are purely Fictional and any resemblance to actual persons, living or dead, is coincidental.

Printed in the United States of America

This book is dedicated to the loving memory of Gail Sandra Patmon-Wilson-White.
September 22,1947–March 28, 2003

"My past successes and failures are a part of my yesterday, today, and tomorrow"-
Carmen K. Glenn

Indianapolis, Indiana is the perfect city for Victoria Jackson. The city where they drive fast, live fast, and excel even faster. Victoria loves the pace of the city and even moreso loves the pace of her explosive career. The thirty five year old Senior Executive is married to William, a successful partner in a reputable law firm. The happy couple seems to have a perfect life: a strong marriage, two promising careers, and a custom home in the suburbs of Indianapolis. When Victoria graduated with an MBA more than a decade ago, she hoped she would be in this exact position at this exact time in her life, destined to become the first African American female CEO of JDL, the Fortune 500 Marketing Firm. Victoria dreamed she would use her power and prestige to pave the road for other Black females climbing the ladder of success in Corporate America. However Victoria veered from that direction long ago and has become swept up with materialism, power, and competition. As the intensity of the competition spikes, Victoria begins to display physical symptoms of the tremendous stress. Still, her desire to succeed never waivers. Nothing can stand in Victoria's way of becoming CEO, except feelings erupting with a new member of the executive team. Ride along with Victoria as her detour with the handsome and devilish co-worker heats up. Will Victoria put the breaks on in time to salvage her marriage and career or will she crash and burn?

SEPTEMBER

Chapter 1

Victoria

Late for work again. I especially hate to be late for a meeting when I know I am going to be the only black person there. Living down the stereotype of Colored People's Time puts a lot of stress on a woman. I always try to make a good impression on the job and punctuality is a key point. I feel my armpits begin to perspire, although I have the air conditioning fan blasting on the highest level. I turn up the volume on my car stereo to hear Tom, Myra, Sybil and Jay on the morning show over the sound of the blowing air. I speed up my BMW to seventy miles per hour on route I-465. "Lord, please don't let me get another speeding ticket." I give it a second thought and I slow down to 60 mph. Now, I start weaving through morning traffic.

If William were in the car he would say, "I know this is Indianapolis, but you are not in the Indianapolis 500!" This morning if I were in the race I would place at least in the top ten. Traffic jam! I slow down and force my way out of the fast lane into the outside lane.

As I reach the inner city, I decide to take my chances on an alternate route. I make a hard right turn at the traffic light. I punch on the gas pedal. I am driving at top speed on the downtown streets. I make a hard left at the next traffic light and bingo! I hit green lights for seven blocks! Okay, just a few more blocks. I stop at a red light. I listen as DJ Jay Anthony murders another song as he sings along to a Top 40 hit over the sound waves. I laugh out loud and tap on the steering wheel to the beat of the music.

Finally, the light turns green and I take off leaving tread marks and smoke behind. After just a few blocks, I hit another red light. Now the morning show group has decided to play a little theme music for the rush hour travelers. A little "Move Get Out Tha Way" is just what I need. I usually treat my downtown commute as a competition. Each day I try to beat my time from the previous day. Finally, I see the checkered flag and I complete the last block of the race. Today my time is exceptional. Eat your heart out, Danica!

As I make a right turn down into the sub-basement parking garage, I lower the volume of the loud rap music blaring from my stereo. It is time for me to turn off my world and get into the groove of the corporate lifestyle I have chosen for myself. JDL, the Fortune 500 Marketing Firm, is where I spend all of my days and most of my nights.

I grab my briefcase and hustle out of the car. "Feet don't fail me now," I say to myself as I jog the distance to the parking garage elevator. It is only 7:15 am and it is already hot and humid, a typical Indy summer morning. Thank goodness the end of summer is nearing. I think about the weather cooling off and autumn approaching as my shirt begins sticking to my back after just a few steps. I hope my hair spray holds up. I must look like quite a sight. It is not everyday you see an immaculately dressed black woman running through this parking garage with her hair flying behind her. This would be so much easier if I had on some of those tennis shoes many of the downtown female professionals wear to and from the office, but I would never be caught dead looking so tacky. I reach the parking garage elevator and go up to the main floor.

I walk quickly through the lobby of my office building, knowing marble floors and three-inch pumps do not mix. I wait impatiently for the elevator and after two attempts I squeeze onto an already crowded elevator. It does not feel like the air conditioning is working in here at all. It also smells like someone's deodorant has not made it through the morning rush hour. Automatically I look up and peek at the weight capacity. I start praying. A man weighing at least four hundred pounds gets off on the second floor and I think we all breathe a sigh of relief. I make it to the nineteenth floor.

The nineteenth floor is my domain. The Research and Planning Division of JDL has been my life for the last five years. As Senior Executive of Research, I rule the division with an iron fist. I expect perfection and I have no tolerance for those who cannot deliver. Long work hours are expected and a fast and furious pace is the norm. Applicants searching for a nine-to-five monotonous work schedule need not apply.

As I depart from the elevator, I feel my subordinate staff shutter. The noise level drops by several octaves when they see me coming. Employees who were only seconds ago standing around the water cooler disperse into the maze of cubicles as I approach. Those who were leisurely sipping on coffee sit their cups down and begin to peck away at their keyboards as I move through the workstations. I acknowledge those who are brave enough to make eye contact with me with a nod and very professional greeting as I aggressively walk to my office.

"Good morning Maryann."

"Good morning Mrs. Jackson."

"Good morning Roger."

"Good morning Mrs. Jackson."

"Good morning James."

"Top of the morning to you Mrs. Jackson."

I like James.

I see Malcolm Prince, the newest Senior Executive walking towards me. He is a tall, dark, and handsome brother. Malcolm is an ex-football player. I do not know how long he has been out of the game, but the man still has the body of a Greek god. Malcolm is perfectly dressed, as usual. From the top of his head, to the bottom of his feet, he is pure perfection. His hair is perfectly faded, teeth are straight and perfectly white, and his nails are obviously manicured. His suit, shirt, tie and shoes are definitely designer items too (underwear and socks probably included). I know he is married, although he does not wear a wedding band. Malcolm is a big flirt.

Malcolm sees me and rushes my way.

"Good morning Victoria. How are you?" he asks, grinning with those perfect white teeth.

"Hello Malcolm," I say, smiling in return. "I'm doing just fine. Unfortunately, I'm running a little late this morning." I try to sound like I regret not being able to talk to him, when I could really care less.

Malcolm walks directly up to me, invading my personal space. I like to keep people at least two arm lengths away. I hate for people, especially men, to brush up against me even in crowded spaces. Malcolm towers over my five foot nine inch frame even in three-inch pumps. I get a strong whiff of his cologne and it smells heavenly— strong and manly. It makes my heart beat fast. Malcolm leans in so closely; we are practically nose-to-nose. He speaks in a smooth baritone croon. I hold my breath as he talks.

"Victoria I've been trying to schedule a meeting with you for two days. When can we get together?"

I take two steps backward and not as smoothly as I hoped. I nearly trip over my feet as I search for a smooth, yet definite put off. "I'm sorry Malcolm. It's just that things have been rather hectic. You know how it is. Why don't you give my secretary, Maxine, a call and schedule some time for us to get together?"

"That sounds great. Don't let me hold you up. I'll catch up with you later," he says and begins to back away.

"Sure Malcolm," I say. All the while I am thinking, "Whatever." I hurry along and hope I was not smiling too hard at the handsome devil. Besides, what is Malcolm doing on the nineteenth floor this morning anyway? His department is not included in the morning meeting. I wonder why he is here so early.

I try to dash pass my secretary, Maxine Rogers. "Good morning, Max," I say. She does not let me get away with this. Now Max, she is a trip. She is a fifty-three year old divorced black woman from the east coast with a lot of attitude. She describes herself as a "retired hoochie". It is hard not to give Max attention. She demands it. She wears her hair in a platinum blond mini-afro style; she has a gold tooth in the front of her mouth. The blonde and gold do not blend well with her dark skin tone. To top things off her outfits tend to be extremely unusual. Today Max has on all light pink. She is a big girl and it makes her look like the Easter Bunny.

What I like most about Max is she makes it her business to stay apprised of what is going on at all levels at JDL. Lucky, for me, Max and I became fast friends five years ago. In fact, Max practically welcomed me with open arms when I came to JDL. She had been the only black person on the nineteenth floor with the research staff for six months. She felt she had worked her way up the ladder of success and out of the Black world she is so comfortable in. Max feels extremely uncomfortable in the "European World", as she calls it. When I asked her why she continues to sacrifice her comfort level to work in Corporate America, she said she does not have to sleep with one eye open anymore.

Max and I have a give-and-take relationship. I give Max gifts for her birthday, Secretary's Day, and Christmas. In return, Max keeps me informed of everything I need to know about what goes on at JDL. Sometimes, Max goes too far with her information. Oh well, there is really no such thing as TMI (Too Much Information).

"Good morning, Ms. Thing," Maxine whispers. Between Max and I we like to try to keep it real.

"Max you are too much," I scold her jokingly.

Max giggles. She then leans over her desk and says, "Make sure you fix your weave before you go in. You look like you flew in on an airplane with the windows down this morning."

"Thanks, girlfriend," I say gratefully. I turn and make a mad dash for the executive restroom adjoined to my office. I hurriedly refresh my lipstick and comb through my wind blown hair. Maxine knows my hair is real, but she refers to it as my "weave", because she knows it cracks me up. I survey myself quickly in the mirror. "Perfect. If I do say so myself." I selected the perfect navy blue designer ensemble for my power meeting this morning. The outfit is made complete with a pair of navy blue shoes and a navy blue briefcase. I tell myself, "Knock 'em dead."

And I do.

As we exit the morning meeting, CEO Bernard Rich asks me to meet with him in his office in fifteen minutes. I am not surprised. I really showed off this morning and I am due a few accolades for my performance today.

Fourteen minutes later I take the steps from the nineteenth floor to the twentieth floor. I think to myself how much I will enjoy

coming to the twentieth floor one day. This will be my domain. I will
be the "Ruler of JDL", "The Queen B". I look around and imagine a
few feminine touches added to the large waiting area belonging to the
CEO's office. I will definitely show off more of my personal style
when this place belongs to me. I take one look at the twenty-five year
old blonde secretary with the double D breast implants and stiletto
heels. Maxine says she is compensated handsomely for her skills per-
formed under the CEO's desk. I make a mental note to terminate her
during my acceptance speech. Maxine has always looked out for a sister, so I will bring her to the twentieth floor with me.

I walk straight up to the big-breasted secretary and smile,
"Good morning, Catherine."

Catherine looks up from the Motherhood magazine she is
reading. Her job must be really tough. "Good morning, Mrs. Jackson.
Mr. Rich is expecting you, go right in."

I laugh to myself and say, "Thanks." I open the door to the
CEO's office wider than necessary, but the added effect seems to go
with how I am feeling today. I am on top of the world.

Mr. Rich looks up from his computer monitor as I enter and
promptly invites me to have a seat on the other side of his desk. He is
a large balding man of the majority persuasion. I quickly make myself
comfortable in the black masculine leather high back chair. I smile
and put on my game face. Mr. Rich clears his throat, which he does
every time before he speaks. I try to look him straight in the eye. My
eyes tend to focus on his overly trimmed moustache, which makes
him look like a super-sized Hitler. Mr. Rich gets right to the point.

"Jackson, I have asked to speak with you today, because I want
to apologize for what happened yesterday during the stakeholders
meeting."

I know exactly which incident Mr. Rich is speaking of. I let
him go on.

"The male attitude around here towards women and their
place in this organization is prehistoric. I am ashamed of how some of
the men around here have acted and the words they have chosen to
use. I want you to know I don't support their ignorance. Women have
always held an important position in this organization. I built this
company from the ground up and I built it to include everyone who
has the guts and the drive to support this company's mission. Gender

does not matter here. It never has."

"Mr. Rich it is not necessary for you to apologize because the word 'bitch' was used in a meeting yesterday. I believe I thoroughly handled the situation."

"You're correct, you certainly did handle the situation. You handled it appropriately and with a great deal of class, as you handle all matters."

"Thank you Mr. Rich."

"I just can not for the life of me understand why a woman who is assertive, professional, and strong-willed is consistently referred in a derogatory manner."

Silence. I provide no response. Mr. Rich sits quietly before he starts in again.

"How do you think that prehistoric group would refer to a man with the same characteristics: assertive, professional, and strong?"

This time I do not hesitate, but I jump right in with a response. "Sir, I believe they would call him a 'leader'."

"But why does there have to be a difference?"

"Sir, I know it's the year 2005, but in many ways our society's attitudes and values have not changed as much as some of us would like to think."

"You're right."

I tire of this discussion. I have had this same discussion with other female colleagues my entire professional career. This subject may be new to Mr. Rich, a millionaire Caucasian male, but this is old business to me. I started my career working twelve-hour days seven days a week just to prove myself as an equal in this male-dominated society I chose to work in, also known as Corporate America. Sometimes I wonder why I even bother. But when I think about it, I know why I do what I do. It is because I am good at it. No, I am great at it.

"Jackson there is one more thing. I wanted you to be the first to hear the news. This morning I notified the Board of Directors of my intent to retire at the end of this year. I will be making a recommendation to the Board for my replacement in the weeks to come."

Inside I am jumping for joy. He is leaving! Now it is my chance! It is time for me to arrive! It is time for me to be on top! Inside I am smiling, but I try to contain myself and extend my congratulations to Mr. Rich on his retirement. I manage to also express my humble gratitude for his years of guidance.

Chapter 2

Bernard

*F*or thirty years I have devoted my life to JDL. I built this company from the ground floor. I have poured my heart and soul into this company to make it is what it is today. I have sacrificed every-thing—my relationship with my wife and kids, my health, and my spirit. I can no longer keep up with the game. I have struggled with the tech-nology for more than the last decade. I have enjoyed my time here, but now my time is over. Until just a few months ago, I was a sixty five year old washed up has been. Then I found love.

For me, love came in the form of a twenty five year old temp sec-retary. Catherine and I have been seeing each other privately since the first day of her temp assignment with JDL. I am completely in love with her. I realize Catherine may be my last chance at happiness. I am not too old and too foolish to know she would not give an old fat bald man like me a chance if it were not for the millions of dollars I have in the bank. Still I love her.

My wife thinks in January after my retirement we will move to Florida and live happily ever after in a boring retirement community. My three adult kids think my retirement means one step closer to the grave *and one step closer to them getting their hands on my money. Well, they're all wrong. I have no desire to waste away in Florida surrounded by a bunch of old farts. I want to live!*

So instead, at the end of December, Catherine and I are running away to Mexico. There we can get married and raise our child together. The child Catherine has inside of her has sparked a sense of hope in me that I did not realize was still alive. Catherine and this baby are my last chance for real love.

Chapter 3

Victoria

"The meeting today was awesome," I say to William. I can tell he is smiling on the other end of the telephone.

"That's good, baby. I can't wait to hear all about it tonight," he replies. "I'll be leaving the office in an hour and I'll meet you at home," he adds. It is already seven o'clock in the evening. William is a partner at one of the most reputable law firms in Indianapolis and he always works late. We have a half-a-dozen of these brief cell phone conversations throughout our long days.

"But you haven't heard the best part yet."

"What's that sweetheart?"

"Bernard Rich announced his retirement to the Board of Directors this morning, effective the end of this year. The CEO always makes a recommendation to the Board for their replacement."

"That's great news Vic. You know you have the CEO position in the bag."

"I don't know, William. There is still David Tray to contend with. He's been the JDL golden boy for years."

"Tray is no competition for you."

"I think Tray is my biggest competitor for the position. He came up through the ranks in JDL. Although I am a Senior Executive, I have only been with JDL for five years. Despite Tray's complete inability to perform his duties, JDL has continued to recognize and promote that idiot."

"Well I think he has reached his final level of incompetence. Tray is definitely not CEO material."

"Well thanks for your vote of confidence." Personally, I think William is exactly right about David Tray. He has faked his way through Corporate America for far too long. He talks a good game, but he cannot produce results. Still, he suffers the white male syndrome of being able to advance despite lacking the appropriate job skills. His Ivy League education and family connections have gotten him where he is today. Intellect and job knowledge played no part in his success.

William pauses and goes right to his next line of business. "You didn't forget you have to talk with Maria when you get home, did you?"

"No William I didn't forget. I remember our discussion," I grumble. "I'll see you at home." I end the conversation abruptly.

William is referring to our discussion about our maid, Maria. This will be my second discussion with Maria about the dry cleaning. Twice she has neglected to pick up the clothes from the dry cleaners. Overall, I like having Maria around. She cleans, does the laundry and cooks dinner for us each weekday. Prior to us getting Maria we rarely had a home cooked meal. Maria and I have had a number of talks over the past year. She shared with me her family history. She came to the United States from Mexico when she was just a young girl. She has worked as a domestic most of her life. She has four adult children, two girls and two boys. She is a grandmother to seven grandchildren. Her husband retired last year for health reasons. He has been under medical care for some time now. Since his employer does not provide health coverage, the medical bills have mounted, which is why she came to work for us.

I pick up my cell phone and dial Max's home telephone number. She answers quickly and obviously she sees my number on her caller id.

"Yes, how may I help you?" she asks with an attitude.

"Drop the attitude. I have major JDL news."

"What happened?"

"Bernard Rich has announced his retirement effective the end of the year. He has to make a recommendation to the Board of Directors to replace him."

"What?"

"You heard me right!"

"Richie Rich is on his way out the door and my girl is moving on up like the Jeffersons. There is no other Senior Exec more competent and capable of becoming the next CEO. The bottom line is JDL would be nothing without Victoria Jackson!"

I laugh hysterically. Max is crazy. "Max first of all you need to stop referring to Bernard Rich as Richie Rich before you slip up and call the man Richie at work. Besides what makes you and William both assume I will be the next CEO?"

"Really Victoria you should stop being so modest. You have the position hands down. There is honestly no other competition"

"Well thanks for your vote of confidence Max."

"Besides you have to get the promotion, because I need a raise."

"Max that's just like you to think about yourself."

"Well, my mama didn't raise no fool. When you go up the ladder, I go up the ladder too."

"Max you're absolutely right. Any progress for me means progress for you."

My phone makes a soft "beep-beep" sound.

"Max, let me go. I have another call coming in."

"I'll see ya tomorrow, Ms. CEO."

"Bye, Max."

I click over and take the other call. It's a bill collector. The American Express account payment is late again and there will be a high late fee assessed to the account.

"What else is new?" I hang up on the minimum wage caller.

I continue to drive on automatic pilot for the forty-minute commute to the suburbs from downtown. I pull into our four-car garage. I start to think about my pending discussion with Maria. I walk inside and hear her in the kitchen with the television on loudly.

I smell smoke. As I continue to move forward the smell of smoke becomes stronger. Something is definitely burning. Smoke is everywhere! I drop my purse and briefcase and rush into the kitchen. Maria is sitting on a barstool with her elbows resting on the counter and her chin resting in her hand. Smoke is spewing from the stove.

"What the hell is going on?" I shout.

I startle Maria out of her trance. She jumps up and nearly falls off the kitchen stool.

"Huh, what?" Maria asks.

The smoke detector goes off and the sound is absolutely outrageous. I hurry to the stove and turn it off. I open several of the kitchen windows.

"Oh no! Let me take care of that for you, Ms. Victoria", Maria says. "I just looked away for one minute and I don't know what happened," she explains.

Maria pulls out the burnt piece of meat from the oven and dumps it into the kitchen sink. She begins to fan the smoke from the burning mound with a kitchen towel.

"I am so sorry, Ms. Victoria. I will clean up this mess right away."

I am standing with my hands on my hips thinking, "How in the hell do you clean up smoke?" "Maria when you're finished here, I'll see you in the study!" I yell over the smoke detector.

I suppose my voice would be raised even if the smoke detector were not blaring. My temper is flared just as high as the burnt dinner. I storm off into the study. I pace the floor for several minutes before I am able to calm myself enough to sit down. I try to get my mind off the fact that the entire house is filled with smoke and smells horribly. I open several more windows and light a scented candle on my desk. Once the smoke detector stops and the pleasant aroma begins to fill the room, I begin to relax enough to attend to my evening work. I pick up the stack of mail delivered today. There is a post card from Hawaii with a clear picture of a beach and a blue sky. I turn the post card over to the back and I read it. It is from our friends, Phillip and Monique Robinson.

Phillip Robinson and William have been best friends since law school. Monique Robinson and I have become good friends over the years. Phillip and Monique's relationship blossomed along side the relationship William and I developed. For years we double dated, went on vacations together and were quite close. Monique and I spent hours on the telephone weekly sharing the details of our relationships. However, over the years our lives have taken a very different course. Phillip Robinson maintains a private law practice and Monique is the part time secretary in his office. They own a modest home in the inner city of Indianapolis where they live with their three children all under the age of four. Monique is quite content as her husband's secretary and her role as mother. Their lives are filled with preschool, diapers, and breastfeeding. What a waste. Monique is such an intelligent woman. I will never understand for the life of me why Monique plays second fiddle to her husband. She has given up her entire life to fulfill the desires of her man.

We had a nice vacation with Phillip and Monique last summer in Hilton Head. This year they invited William and I to join them in Hawaii, but my hectic schedule at JDL does not leave much time to get away. In addition, William's busy schedule at the firm keeps him working late most nights and weekends. In fact, it has been some time since we have been able to spend time with the Robinsons. It seems William and I seldom have time for friends anymore. Unless we pencil in an engagement on our calendar, our schedules permit practically no time for socializing. We go to lots of "affairs", but they are typically career related. There have been dozens of private parties for the partners at the firm. There is always some celebration for securing a lucrative client or bonuses for billing outrageous hours. William and I both enjoy these gatherings. Networking is key for both of us. In fact, I made my current career connection at one of the firm's gatherings five years ago. I walked in the party with a black velvet evening gown and my million-dollar smile. I walked out just a few hours later with the promise of a position that raised me to a six-figure salary.

Maria walks into the study, breaking my concentration and announces, "Dinner will be ready in just a few minutes Miss Victoria. Will Mr. William be arriving home shortly?"

I do not reply to her question. Instead I bark out, "Maria sit down." Maria sits down slowly. She is clearly uncomfortable. This does not stop the shrewd businesswoman from coming out in me. I speak sternly. "Maria I have been less than satisfied with your performance the last few weeks. This evening you could have burned the

entire house down. Your total disregard for our home is unforgivable.
I am going to have to let you go."

Maria is in total disbelief. "Oh, I'm so sorry Miss Victoria. I
have been very happy working for you and Mr. William."

I am not in the mood for excuses. I seldom am. I have fired
dozens of employees over the years for lesser offenses than what Maria
committed today. I look into Maria's eyes. She is just another dis-
pensable servant. Maria sees the look on my face. She reads it well,
but decides to attempt to pull on my heartstrings.

"I don't know what I'm going to do to take care of me and my
sick husband, Miss Victoria."

"Maria you will have to talk to the agency about that problem."

"I understand," Maria says. She hangs her head and begins to
walk out of the room.

I stand motionless, while she walks through the kitchen, gath-
ers her belongings, and walks out the back door. I return to my task
of sorting through today's mail. There is a letter from Ohio, several
credit card bills, and a ton of utility bills. I open the bills. The two
credit card bills are at the maximum limit but the utilities, for the
most part, are current. This has been the typical state of our financial
affairs and a source of strain between William and me.

We built our custom home nearly three years ago. The project
was more expensive than we budgeted. In the past three years we have
filled the house with all of the modern conveniences and this has put
a tremendous stress on our finances even with our healthy income.
The money seems to go so fast. I worked myself into a frenzy when
we moved into our house to make it into a home fit for a successful
law partner and business professional. In one weekend, preparing for
our first small dinner party, I set out to make the appropriate pur-
chases. I shopped for an entire week to select the finishing touches. I
had a couple of oriental rugs, china, and stemware delivered to the
house. William threw a complete fit when he found out I extended
the credit limit on two of our cards. That was our first official fight
over money. Unfortunately, it was not the last. At some point, I
should sit down and refigure our budget. I prefer to do this task alone.
William will take one look at our budget and cut out all of my extravagant expenses. If I do the budget, I can slash all of his extravagant

expenses. I will attend to the budget soon, but not tonight. I decide instead to take the letter to the bedroom to read. I stand up to close the windows. Suddenly, I see stars. I cannot catch my breath...I stumble and reach for a nearby chair...I miss the chair and continue to stumble. After what seems like several minutes, when in reality it has only taken a few seconds, I hit the floor. My mind fades to black...

Chapter 4

Maria

I cannot believe she just fired me after all I have done for her. I have gone above and beyond the call of duty for William and Queen Victoria Jackson. How could she dare accuse me of not respecting her home? Heck, I have been there with them since the day they moved into the "Jackson Castle". I remember the day of the move in like it was yesterday. The house was empty on moving day, even after the moving truck left. I could not understand why the couple needed a housekeeper. The moving truck dropped off several boxes filled with clothing and accessories belonging to Queen Victoria and a ton of law books belonging to William. That was it. It did not take long however, for the Queen to start filling up the castle with department store furniture and knick-knacks from QVC. There were delivery trucks arriving daily. The UPS man and I became close personal friends. Jim was his name. I saw Jim more than my husband in those days.

Now I have to go home to my drunken husband, Enrico, and tell him his liquor money has been temporarily cut off until I get a new gig. Most weeks he starts drinking on Friday night and does not finish until Monday morning. It takes him a few days to sober up so he can start all *over again. Enrico is the reason our four children do not come to visit me anymore. They hate to see their Papi drunk. Well, their Papi was good enough for them when he was paying their way through college and trade school. He was a drunk then, too. Now that they are all grown up and professionals living in big houses, their Papi's drinking is an embarrassment to them. So I am left to deal with Enrico by myself. Thank goodness, up to this point, I have been able to maintain our two-bedroom apartment. When Enrico starts his drunken rages, I lock myself into my bedroom with a heavy padlock. I have cable TV, a mini refrigerator, and a microwave in my bedroom. I can stay in there all weekend with the bucket in the corner as my toilet.*

If Enrico gives me any lip tonight, there is going to be some domestic violence in our apartment. This time he will be the one to walk away with two black eyes. Besides, who is he to talk bad to me any way? Enrico has not held a job in the last decade. It has been me that has maintained us in the manner in which we have become accustomed , a pitiful two-bedroom apartment on the south side of town. The heat does not always work in the winter and the air conditioning unit does not always cool in the summer. Still, we have a roof over our heads and food on the table— even if the food is leftovers from the Jackson castle. I bring home the bacon and serve it up every night, while Enrico eats, drinks, and then passes out on the couch.

Today, I know I was wrong for getting wrapped up in the television and burning dinner. Most days a good TV show is all I have to look forward to. I can forget about my own depressing life with Enrico and imagine that I am very far away and standing in someone else's shoes. Every single day at "The Castle" is the same ol', same ol' and basically I was getting tired of it anyway. If I give it a second thought, I am actually relieved. I was tired of traveling clear across town to work for slave wages for Queen Victoria. Everyday she would leave me a posted note on the refrigerator with one or two extra tasks to complete that were not in our agreement. I was tired of staying late because she was working late and she wanted her dinner warm and on the table when she arrived. I was tired of coming in on Saturdays for brunches and cocktail parties for phony business people. The woman does not have a single real friend to invite to her parties.

The Queen never cooks, the Queen never lifts a finger around her own house, and the Queen would not know a good thing if it jumped up and slapped her in the face! All that woman knows how to do is work for that stupid company. That is all I hear about, "JDL" this and "JDL" that. If I never hear the combination of those three letters again, I will die a happy woman. I know every detail of every employee at that stupid place. If I have to hear about one more product that stupid company is marketing, I think I will lose my mind.

I do not believe she knows the first thing about being a proper wife to Mr. William. Now, he is a handsome and quality man. Mr. William is the real reason I have stayed at the Jackson home so long. If the man has any sense, he will run from the Queen as fast as his feet will carry him. He deserves a wife, who will give him a reason to come home at night. Mr. William deserves a woman who will make him some pretty brown babies. He deserves a wife who will take more time on their marriage than working to become the CEO of JDL. I would not be surprised if some of those late nights at "the firm" is time spent away with a real woman. I can just see Mr. William in a cozy little restaurant hugged up with a beautiful woman. I hope he has some happiness in his life outside of "The Castle".

In fact, I have a good mind to call Mr. William at the firm and tell him what his wife has done to me. No, forget it. I refuse to work another day in that house with that punta!

Chapter 5

Victoria

I hear William's voice, but I cannot hear what he is saying. I am asleep. He is shaking me.

"Vic can you hear me? Are you alright?" William is speaking very loudly.

I open my eyes, but I cannot say anything. I try to shake my head in the affirmative, but that is a very bad idea. I apparently have a splitting headache. I manage to place my hand on my head and I begin to moan. William is standing over me and he looks like he just saw a ghost.

"Oh baby, what happened? Should I dial 9-1-1?"

"No," I mutter.

"What happened?"

I try to pull myself up to a sitting position, but I require William's assistance. "I'm not sure," I say just above a whisper.

"You're not sure how you ended up on the floor?" He is still speaking very loudly.

"No. Wait a minute." It is starting to come back to me. "The last thing I remember is Maria leaving after I fired her."

"You fired Maria? I just asked you to talk to her, not fire the woman!"

"Honey this is not the time for an argument. Just help me up," I manage to say.

William helps me to my feet and guides me carefully up the long winding staircase and into the bedroom. He lays me gently on the four-poster king-size bed. William goes into the restroom and I hear him turn the water on to the faucet. The water goes off and quickly he brings out a cool wet towel.

"Just what happened with Maria?" he asks, as he places the wet towel on my head.

"Aren't you concerned about me?"

"Of course I am sweetheart," he says tenderly. "This whole situation has caught me off guard. First, I come home to find you lying on the floor and non-responsive. Secondly, all you say you remember is firing the maid. I'm more than concerned. I am going to call Dr. Brown and ask that she make a house call."

"Look baby I'm fine. My head hurts, but I'm sure I'll be okay. It's really not necessary to call Dr. Brown," I insist.

"Ok, but promise me you'll go into Dr. Brown's office tomorrow."

"I will. I promise." I mean it.

"Now can you tell me what happened with Maria?"

"William, it's no big deal. I came home and found the entire house filled with smoke. Maria was just sitting around watching the TV in the kitchen while the dinner was in flames inside the oven. The smoke detector went off. She was so wrapped up in what was going on with one of those stupid reality TV shows, she almost let the entire house burn down. Anyway, she left something else in the kitchen for dinner, so go help yourself honey."

"The house almost burned down? That sounds like some exaggeration," William chuckles.

"Unless you are representing Maria in a unjustifiable employment termination suit, I suggest you get over it William! The woman was royally screwing up and I had had enough. I talked to her just last week about her not picking up the clothes from the drycleaners. She repeated the same mistake again this week. Today I came home to find the house full of smoke and dinner a disaster. Let's not forget about the incident with the cats. Remember the day you came home early and she had three stray cats in the kitchen? I refuse to have our 1.2 million dollar home infested with fleas and plagued with pet odor!"

William laughs, "You can not treat the housekeeper like one of the high-priced employees at JDL. We barely paid Maria above minimum wage and you expect a lot of work for very little pay."

"I know exactly how much money we paid Maria. Maria was hired help and I expect good customer service. She could not deliver, so she's gone. It's as simple as that."

William continues to laugh. He leans over the bed and kisses me on the forehead. I hate it when he does that. It makes me feel like a child. I know he does it on purpose.

"You will have to call the agency for a new housekeeper right away. Since you do all the firing, I'll leave it up to you, sweetheart, to hire a new maid."

I do not dignify William's statement with a response. Instead I get out of the bed and get two aspirin and a glass of water for my headache. William heads to the kitchen for dinner. I head to the study to retrieve the unopened letter. I find the letter lying on the floor in the study. I knew from the moment I laid eyes on it that it is from my baby brother in Ohio.

My baby brother has been in prison for the last eighteen years for manslaughter. Last year, he went before the parole board and begged for his release. He was denied. I was not there when it happened. I have never gone to see him in prison. I do not think I can tolerate seeing my baby brother caged up like an animal. It makes me feel weak knowing my baby brother is stuck in prison and there is nothing I can do to get him out. Not my money, my connections, or my job can influence his release. I hate to feel so powerless.

****

Work is intense the next day. I love it. I am good at what I do and everybody knows it. It is apparent to everyone that I come in contact with that I am one hundred percent committed to my career. I spend countless hours researching and preparing for projects. I volunteer for every committee and additional assignment. I know the entire list of who's who in the marketing world. I love to walk into a meeting and demand everyone's attention. I love to outshine the latest newcomer. I love to show off my intellect. There is a part of me that loves attention. I know that is a part of the reason I married William. William is the oldest of four children and the only boy. His mother and three sisters taught him well how to spoil a woman. Growing up the only girl with five brothers made me demand attention from the opposite sex. Lucky for me my field is dominated by men.

Men are easy to manipulate. All it takes is a big smile, a nice body, and a flip of the hair to get their attention. A little cleavage never hurts either. There hasn't been a man I have encountered that I cannot have eating out of my hand in five minutes. I am that good. I do not try to hide my skills. Men appreciate the obvious. They like a woman who knows she is all that and a bag of chips. I do not mind allowing them to think they are my "friend" or they have some kind of inside track. The bottom line is that I get what I want out of the deal. I always want information. One can never know too much information about a co-worker. You never know when you might have to use it against them.

My favorite is meeting a co-worker after work for drinks. One would be surprised at the type of information men share with me. When men are away from the office in a casual setting, they gossip more than any group of women. They seem to believe we are talking "off the record". One thing I learned very early in my career is that everything you say is "on the record" and if you do not want someone to know something "don't tell anyone" and that includes your own mama.

I am on the fast track to success. I am thirty-five years old. I have an MBA and I earn a six-figure salary. I am employed by a Fortune 500 company. The only way for me to go from here is up. I am committed to maintaining all of the facets of a successful professional. I have the designer clothes, the foreign car, the custom-built home in the suburbs, and even the successful husband to complete the package. In fact, William's ambition is one of the reasons I married him seven years ago. We were both madly in love and full of ambition. William loves to work just like I do. We are in most ways a perfect couple. There is only one thing we disagree about: children.

William thinks there is room for children in our lives. I disagree. In fact, William feels so passionately about this subject, he negotiated the terms of our parenthood on our wedding night. He insisted we have two children and I insisted we have none. We negotiated and settled on one child. William actually wrote a post-nuptial agreement that night and I signed it. He reminds me that I have failed to live up to the terms and condition of our marital contract every chance he gets. I pretend that I have amnesia. Every wedding anniversary William actually pulls out the written agreement. I protest that I was under the influence of alcohol on our wedding night (I consumed a half bottle of champagne at our wedding reception). Still, every year, it is getting more and more difficult to put him off. William and my gynecologist tell me my biological clock is ticking, but I do not hear a thing.

Chapter 6

Victoria

After work, I drive to Dr. Brown's office. Dr. Brown has been my physician the entire time I have lived in Indianapolis. I like her. She seems to be a lot like me. She is knowledgeable in her field, she is a hard worker, she is brief and to the point. I do not care that she does not have much of a bedside manner. I do not have time for idle chitchat. Dr. Brown is as concerned about the passing out episode as I am. She forces me to submit to a pregnancy test despite my insistence I have never missed a single birth control pill since I was eighteen years old. Like I said, she seems a lot like me, bossy. After Dr. Brown rules out pregnancy, she insists we review my family medical history.

Dr. Brown sits on the tiny circular chair on rollers. She pushes her tiny wire rimmed glasses up her tiny nose, so she can see my electronic file on the PC sitting on top of the small desk inside the small examination room. Dr. Brown wastes no time asking questions. "Do you have a family history of any of the following: mental illness?"

"Yes"

"Who?"

"My aunt."

"Maternal or paternal?"

"Maternal."

"Depression?"

"Yes."

"Who?" This time Dr. Brown looks over her small wire rimmed glasses as if she is becoming inpatient with my less than thorough answers already.

"My mother."

"Anxiety?"

"Yes, my paternal aunt." Now, I've got the hang of it.

"High Blood Pressure?"

"Yes, my father, both of my grandfathers and all five of my brothers." Isn't this prevalent in the black community? I thought she was smart.

"Diabetes?"

"Yes, my mother." Isn't this one prevalent too?

"Cancer?"

"No." I don't know why I lie.

"In the last six months have you experienced any of the following symptoms: migraines?"

"Yes."

"Headaches?"

"Constantly."

"Fatigue?"

"Yes"

"Tightness in chest?"

"Yes."

"Joint pain?"

"Yes."

"Aching muscles?"

"Yes."

This time Dr. Brown rips her little glasses completely of her thin nose, presses her lips together tightly and takes a deep breath before asking, "Stomach pain?"

"Yes."

She does the same facial movement before asking, "Blurred vision?"

"Yes after long hours on the computer."

This time she speaks loudly, "Abnormal menstrual periods?"

"No." (I finally found something to truthfully say "no" to!)

At this point, Dr. Brown has lost all patience. Her hair that seemed so neat in a tight old-fashioned bun sitting on top of her tiny head suddenly appears to be coming loose and most of it seems to be standing straight up. She practically yells out, "Victoria you are an absolute mess! What has taken you so long to get in here?"

I do not appreciate Dr. Brown's outburst and I try my best to remain calm. I try to explain, "I am a very busy person and I do not have time to stop everything I am doing for every little ache, pain, and discomfort." I try my best to keep the irritation out of my voice.

"With your tremendous family history you can not afford to let yourself go like this. You are a young woman, but you are experiencing the health problems of a woman much older than your chronological age. This is unacceptable. Victoria you have the means to take better care of yourself and I must insist you do so. It's time for you to get yourself together. I'm almost afraid to ask you about your eating habits."

I guess the look on my face says it all.

Dr. Brown raises her hands up in the air in complete defeat. She stops dealing with me for about three minutes as she furiously types notes into my electronic medical file on the PC.

I sit quietly starring at the petite doctor. She could not be more than four feet and eleven inches. She looks to be in her early fifties and she could not possibly weigh more than ninety pounds. Her tiny fingers are punching away at the keyboard. She stops on two occasions during the three minutes to push her glasses up from the tip of her tiny nose. I try not to move to allow her to concentrate on her task, but with every breath I take, the paper gown seems to make a cracking or scratching sound. I try to hold my breath so the paper will not sound, but the more I try, the more noise I make. Finally I give up. I have an itch behind my left knee. I bend slowly to scratch behind my knee, "crack, crack". I think about what Dr. Brown said to me. I sit and I think, "Forget this witch!"

When Dr. Brown finishes typing, she jumps up from the tiny chair and announces, "I'll be right back, and you can get dressed."

"Thank you," I say sarcastically to the door after she closes it and I give the door the middle finger. I get dressed quickly and I pull out my blackberry from my purse. I've received ten emails already from JDL in the time I have spent in Dr. Brown's office. I reply to them all in the time it takes for Dr. Brown to return.

(1) I am not satisfied. Do it again.
(2) I want the report streamlined.
(3) Wrong, Wrong, Wrong!
(4) What idiot authorized the purchase?
(5) Who died and left him boss?
(6) Have Tech Services fix the laptop in the conference room immediately.
(7) No.
(8) Do not proceed until we can validate the new instrument.
(9) Absolutely not!
(10) What do you mean she is on maternity leave? I did not know she was expecting.

Dr. Brown reenters the examination room and looks at the blackberry in my hand. She frowns again and presses her lips tightly together. This is not a good look for her. "Victoria I suggest you put down the pocket PC. We have serious business to discuss here."

I return the blackberry to my purse and I do my best to give Dr. Brown my full attention.

"Victoria it's time for you to focus on your health." I sit through a ten-minute speech on diet, exercise, and stress reduction. Somewhere in the last thirty seconds of the speech, Dr. Brown manages to squeeze in the fact she believes I recently suffered a panic attack. She gives me the name and number of a therapist she wants me to see. She is clear, direct, and insistent that I follow her recommendation. I walk out hoping she has not charged me extra for the lecture or the bad advice.

I surrender my co-pay at the check out desk near the exit. I walk through the waiting room, out the door and find my car in the parking lot. All the while I am thinking, "How dare she make such a suggestion? Does she really think I am crazy? That is ridiculous. I may be a little stressed out, but who lives without stress? I multi-task, strategize, organize, and prioritize twenty-four hours a day, seven days a week, three hundred sixty-five days a year. I compute, tabulate, and evaluate in my sleep. I think about my list of things to do in the shower every morning. Even when I am sitting on the toilet, I contemplate my next marketing idea. I am a woman driven to succeed. A woman with a purpose. A female on the move. A sister on the go. A bitch on a mission!"

I live a focused life that others, including Dr. Brown, may not readily understand. How could they? Everyone else does not function at my level. I will do things my way. I will reduce my stress and order my own course of treatment—at least temporarily. I have been off my exercise routine. I will go back to the low impact aerobics and kick boxing classes at the health spa. I stopped going three months ago. William thinks it is redundant to have the latest exercise equipment in our home and to pay the exorbitant monthly fees for the exclusive health club we joined. I, of course, disagree with his theory of redundancy. Now that Dr. Brown thinks the stress in my life is so important to relieve, I am willing to go back to the gym. Besides, my body is absolute perfection and there is no cost too great in order to maintain it. I have not gained a pound since I stopped working out, but my body is not as firm as it was. I take a great deal of pride in my appearance. It is an important part of my package. There are a lot of attractive and intelligent sisters out there climbing the ladder of success. However, I stand out in the crowd, because I make it a point to do so. I never leave the house without being completely satisfied with my appearance. Every hair must be in place, every fingernail trimmed and polished, makeup flawless and clothes to die for. I also spare no expense in accomplishing this task.

I did not catch a treasure like William with my intellect alone. He first noticed my rear assets in a tight red dress. My hourglass figure has always gotten me props. Even in my designer suits, my drop dead gorgeous figure shows through and I am not afraid to use it as a weapon. I do not think there is anything wrong with a woman using all her attributes to get ahead. I do whatever it takes to wrap men around my little finger. The combination of brains and beauty is like the effect of a spider sucking the blood out of her catch, rendering them paralyzed. I marvel at seeing them sweat in the boardroom, when I chew them up and spit them out. This has allowed me to go straight to the top of my company. There are a few very smart women who work for JDL, but none can pull the package together like I can. Most other females have average intelligence and average appearance, and that is why their careers are average. Everything about me is exceptional. I have a Senior Executive position and a sought after corner office on the nineteenth floor of JDL. I have only one promotion yet to achieve. That is when everyone will know, Victoria Jackson has arrived.

****

William falls asleep first. He always does. After a long hot shower, I settle into a comfortable pair of pajamas. I head down to the main floor to the study. Partly because I cannot seem to relax tonight and partly because something is on my mind and I can not rest until it is done. I decide it is time to adjust the figures on our budget. I have been putting this off for some time now. It is really not like me to avoid something—even something so unpleasant. I usually take on any challenge straight ahead. Still, this budgeting task is made more difficult, because of the "partnership" of marriage. I jokingly tell myself to simply cut out all of William's extravagant expenses and then the budget will balance! I could cut his private golf lessons, the country club membership including the excessive tab he accumulates every month, and the jazz music collection. I know William works hard and he deserves to play hard too. I sit down and look at the figures reasonably. Both William and I each earn a six-figure salary, but we spend quite excessively. We are a young couple not even in the prime of our careers and earning potential. We have plenty of time to pay off all of this debt. I sit for forty-five minutes and successfully rob Peter to pay Paul. I pay all of the bills on line, at least partially. I even reinstate my membership to the health spa.

I always leave it up to William to mail the check that he sends to his mother in New York. William has been supplementing his mother's income on and off our entire marriage. Right now she is in between husbands again and until her current divorce is settled she is a "little short on cash", as she puts it. Mother Jackson has been married more times than the law should allow. In fact, her four children argue about just how many times she has been married. The oldest daughter says their mother has been married nine times, but the others insist there have only been eight marriages. Whatever the case,

Mother Jackson is a bourgeois, self righteous, pain in the ass. She refuses to talk about how in the world she managed to marry so many times and each time to a millionaire. Mother Jackson says, "A lady does not kiss and tell". Mother Jackson had to be doing something more than a little kissing to catch all of those husbands. She takes every opportunity to share that she has never had relations outside of the sanctity of marriage. She frowns on her youngest daughter, Amber, who is a single mother of a three year old little boy. For that reason alone, Amber is my favorite sister-in-law.

William insists his mother has had a hard life. How he justifies that I do not know. Mother Jackson has never worked a day in her life, unless you count "working it". She has lived in nearly half of the fifty states in the U.S. and three foreign countries. She refers to them as "exotic locations". Mother Jackson has become accustomed to a very high standard of living, which she now depends on William to help her maintain. Quite frankly we can no longer afford to supplement Mother Jackson's income and still remain afloat ourselves. William will notice very quickly when he tries to send Mother Jackson her allowance this month there is nothing left in the account to send.

I climb the staircase and return to the bedroom. I cozy up to a resting William thinking, "Let Mother Jackson go find herself another rich husband, this one is mine." William's body is warm under the plush comforter. He awakes long enough to kiss me gently on the lips and I drift off to sleep. Now, it's William's turn to have trouble falling asleep.

Chapter 7

William

Victoria and I met our senior year in college. She was an undergraduate at Central College in Ohio and I was a student in New York. Her sorority was hosting a spring dance and I was a visiting fraternity brother. All of the sorority sisters wore red flowing evening gowns. Among the numerous pretty girls, Victoria stood out in the crowd. I watched her from a far all night. I tried to get up the nerve to ask her for a dance, but it seemed her dance card was full. Mostly she stepped around with her sorority sisters. She even danced a few slow songs with a couple of different guys. I kept my eye on her while I stepped around and got in a few slow dances myself. I had a few of the Central College girls checking me out, but none sparked my interest like Victoria.

After the dance, the fraternity brothers went to the sorority house for an after party. I tried to play it cool, but I could barely contain myself. I tried desperately to get close to Victoria, realizing this might be my last chance. I watched her as she sat in the living room laughing and socializing with all the others. I decided not to waste any more time and I pulled one of the Ohio frat brothers to the side. I pointed to Victoria and asked him to "hook a brother up". The frat brother was only too happy to *oblige. He was very smooth in his approach. It took him less than sixty seconds to work our way through the room. He waltzed up to Victoria and introduced me. He was so smooth in his technique, I had no problem acting my part and pretending the introduction was not a set up. Victoria stood up and hugged me, which is customary for a brother and sister Greek when meeting for the first time. I was struck by Victoria's dazzling million-dollar smile. Electricity surged throughout my body as I held her close for those few seconds. We stood in place and chatted for a few minutes. My mind was racing. I was desperate to get Victoria to myself. Quickly I made up a game plan. I had to get her alone so I could lay a serious rap on her. I asked Victoria for a drink hoping she would lead me away from the crowd.*

My plan worked. We went to the kitchen for some "purple passion", a specialty drink brewed by the frat brothers. After sipping for a few minutes, Victoria and I found a quiet corner in the house and talked for about an hour amidst all the partygoers. The brothers continued to step and show off for the ladies, while the sisters continued to prance around in their red party dresses. I completely lost myself in Victoria's brown eyes. The party started to heat up about three o'clock am and Victoria and I stepped outside with a few others on the front porch to get a breath of fresh air. I finally worked my way to ask Victoria for her telephone number. Once her digits were secured, I attempted to get a good night kiss, but Victoria averted my efforts. Still, it was all good.

It was two days before I got up the nerve to call Victoria. Her voice was just as lovely on the telephone as she was in person. Much to my disappointment, Victoria told me she had a boyfriend. She said, "we can be friends". That is not what a brother wants to hear when he is trying to get close to a woman as fine as Victoria. Victoria was someone special and I really wanted to get to know her. I was not discouraged. Hell, I had a girlfriend of my own in New York. I was willing to drop her if Victoria would give me a chance. Still, I called Victoria a few times a month and sent her cards for her birthday and Valentines' Day. You could say I was sweating her bad.

Victoria returned my affection for her by doing the same in return. We spent hours on the telephone when we talked in those days. We really had a flow. She insisted that we could really have something if I did not have a girlfriend and she did not have a boyfriend. She also did not like the long distance thing. I thought we could overcome the five hundred miles between us, but she begged to differ. Instead, we maintained a "friendship" for several years.

Victoria called me after college graduation. She told me she had broken up with her boyfriend and would be in Rochester with one of her sorority sisters for the summer. I wined and dined Victoria on my credit card the entire summer she was in town. She was really something special. My favorite part of that summer together was introducing Victoria to my family. My mother and three sisters fell in love with Victoria instantly. Victoria and my youngest sister, Amber, became good friends. While, I clerked at the law firm as a summer intern, Victoria and Amber spent the day shopping and swimming in the pool. It was wonderful coming home after a hard day's work to find Victoria at our house waiting for me. I imagined we were married and I would walk inside the house and announce, "Honey I'm home". Victoria would run to greet me with a hug and kiss. I was in heaven.

I did not mind the fact we did not make love until Victoria's last night in town. I reserved a hotel room for us at one of the finer hotels in town. The package was made complete with a gourmet dinner and champagne served by room service. Victoria and I made love with a passion that I never felt before in my life. I had waited so long to be intimate with her that the pleasure was overwhelming. I stayed awake all night consumed with such love and passion for Victoria. I stroked her hair while she slept. I still recall the moment the sun rose and beamed into the room shinning light on our time together. I hold that mental picture near and dear to my heart to this day.

My best friend Phillip said I was a "chump" and Victoria was playing me, but I disagreed. I was in love with Victoria and I knew it from the first moment I laid eyes on her.

Victoria returned to Ohio for graduate school and I stayed in New York for Law School. We made promises of keeping in touch, but things did not work out for us for years to come. It seemed when I tried to get close to Victoria, she was involved with someone else and when she tried to get close to me, the reverse was true. At one point, Victoria reunited with her college boyfriend and was engaged for about six months. Our long distance love affair struggled.

Much to my surprise, Victoria called me after she ended her first engagement. She had accepted a position in Indianapolis and would be relocating. Finally, I had my chance. I quickly got in touch with my best *friend in Indianapolis and secured a position for myself. I relocated in just a few weeks. I was just so grateful to be near Victoria again. Things were finally working out for Victoria and me. We spent nearly every evening together. Despite Victoria's proclamation of being an independent woman, she spent most of her nights in my bed. Victoria and I dated exclusively for just a few months before we were married.*

Victoria is the love of my life. Sometimes I think I love her more than life itself. I cannot imagine life without her. Lately, I have been scared to death. My wife is not well. The panic attack she suffered concerns me greatly. She has not been herself for a while now. She does not see it in herself, but she has this yearning, this sort of emptiness that she cannot seem to fill. All of the hours she spends working does not fill it. The house, the cars, and all the other things she buys does not fill it. I want to make her happy, but right now I do not know how. This is the first time I have not been able to make things right for Victoria. Whenever Victoria has a problem, I solve it. If she is sick, I nurse her back to health. If her feet hurt, I rub them. If she has a headache, I message her temples. If she needs someone to talk to, I am her best friend and I am right there with a listening ear. If she is sad, I buy her flowers to brighten her day. If she is dissatisfied with her job, I make a few phone calls and arrange for someone to offer her a job at one of the firm's dinner engagements. This has been the basis of our relationship since the beginning. Whenever Victoria was on the rebound or in between relationships, "old stand-in William" was right there to the rescue. Whatever she needs, I give it to her.

This time is different. I cannot tolerate standing by and watching my wife suffer like this. It cuts me deep not to be able to solve this problem for her. If I cannot solve it for her, then I will make sure someone else does. Victoria does not know it, but I have already talked to Dr. Brown about her condition. I know she is going to fight me to the end on this issue; still I will insist she go and see the therapist as Dr. Brown suggested. She will go if I have to take her there myself. I love my wife, but she can be stubborn. Actually, she can be a bitch.

OCTOBER

Chapter 8

Victoria

For three weeks I have avoided Williams insistence I go to see the therapist Dr. Brown recommended. I have also avoided Dr. Brown's phone calls. Caller ID is a beautiful thing. I think I am doing just fine. I have returned to the spa for weekly massages and exercise classes three times a week. I am feeling great. In fact, I think this is the best I have felt in a very long time. William is very pleased with my great mood.

Still, the pressure at JDL is building over the competition for the CEO position. I have had numerous telephone calls from co-workers and even other casual associates about my pursuit for CEO. People are fascinated about the possibility of me becoming the first African-American female to hold the position of CEO at JDL. However, no one is more interested than I. I wish Bernard Rich would make his recommendation and the JDL Board of Directors would make their final decision as well. If I had not been working to reduce my stress anyway, I do not think I would survive.

A few idiots had the nerve to send me emails about the position. They wanted to know if I thought I would get the CEO position. Would I file a civil rights complaint if a white male received the CEO position instead? Did the idiots really expect me to respond on email? Everyone knows email is not confidential. Anyone can obtain an email from cyber space. Even in a legitimate operation like JDL with its built in firewalls and twenty passwords to access the system. I have deleted all of the emails.

Even Max is getting on my last nerve about the CEO competition. She is feeding me rumors from the rumor mill like there is no tomorrow. I cannot slow her down and all of the information is getting me uptight. I just want to scream.

I leave my office because I feel like I need a break and I travel to the eigth floor to speak with Maryann Golden in the Controller's office about fiscal issues for my division. Max tries to stop me on my way out of the door, but I brush pass her like I never saw her open her mouth or raise her hand to motion for me to stop. I make my way to Maryann's office. I arrive outside of Maryann's office only to be stalled by her assistant. Maryann is finishing up a meeting and will be with me in just a few minutes. I think about sitting down, but quickly the two cups of coffee I had this morning have suddenly filled my bladder and I have to pee something awful. I head to the common restroom on the eigth floor. This is something I usually do not do. I prefer to sit my behind on my private toilet when I am at work. Oh well, I will have to stoop over the seat, because I have to use it badly.

I rush in and enter a bathroom stall. I feel like I made it just in time. I am doing my business when I hear the door open and I can barely hear two voices over my steadily flowing stream.

"If they don't hurry up and make an announcement, I think I'll scream."

"I have to know who's going to be running this company, so I can decide if I'm going to stay or not."

"If that black bitch gets this company, the stock will drop at least thirty percent."

The words "black bitch" quickly gain my attention and I instantly stop peeing. I squint and position my head so I can see through the crack of the bathroom stall doors. I see one brown head and one blonde head positioned in front of the mirror.

"More like the stock will drop fifty percent. It'll kill my retirement investments."

"They can't seriously be considering giving it to her."

"Hell no. I heard she had the NAACP here begging the Board of Directors to put her in the CEO position strictly for the publicity of it all. The first black bitch to get the job, bit whoop."

"I heard she had Malcolm X here to vouch for her."

"Sally, Malcolm X is dead."

"Well, it was one of those black panthers: Louis Farrakhan, Martin Luther King, somebody."

Now I want to bust out of this stall and slap the shit out of both of these ignorant bitches. I have not prayed in about six weeks when I last attended church with Monique, but I am praying now. "Lord, give me the strength to stay my behind in this stall and not open up a can of whip ass in this restroom."

"David Tray would make a much better CEO."

"Yes. He's tall, white, and handsome."

The two klanswomen laugh and give each other a high five. Someone walks into the restroom. The two stop talking and the blonde head fluffs her hair while the brown head applies powder to her nose. I can see the intruder is a young black female from where I am half-standing. The two klanswomen say, "Hello Marla."

Marla smiles and says hello to the two klanswomen. Marla you just don't know those two were in here just seconds ago dogging a sister.

Marla enters the stall and begins to do her business. The two klanswomen leave the restroom. I resume peeing. My stream should be red with flames shooting out, because at this time I am boiling mad. I try to shake it off. I descend from the stall, just in time to bump into Marla at the sink washing her hands. Marla looks up and sees me.

"Oh Ms. Jackson. It's so nice to see you again."

"Hello Marla, it's nice to see you too."

Marla seems surprised that I remember her name. The klanswomen were good for something.

"Ms. Jackson I know everyone is talking about the CEO position and I just want you to know I'm rooting for you. Your career has been an inspiration to me. If you become CEO, I'll know it's possible for me to do the same someday."

"Thanks Marla. That's very nice of you. I appreciate you sharing that with me."

Marla dries her hands and walks out of the restroom. Marla does not realize just how much she helped me to shake off the drama from the two klanswomen.

****

"You have a call on line two," says Max.

I stop working on the file on my desk to pick up line two. "Victoria Jackson," I say into the telephone in my best professional tone.

Malcolm Prince responds, "Hello Victoria. What are you doing for lunch today?"

"I don't have any plans Malcolm. What do you have in mind?"

"There's a great Italian restaurant that I would love to take you to," he says.

"That sounds great Malcolm," I respond. "How about noon?"

"I'll meet you in the lobby."

I hang up the telephone with a sly grin on my face. I am not sure why. Malcolm is a handsome man, but I also know his reputation. We have worked together only briefly as Senior Executives, but I have not taken the opportunity to get to know Malcolm very well. Nonetheless, I have avoided his request for a meeting for long enough and now we are finally going to do lunch. Whatever this project he has been bugging me about is, he can finally get it out on the table. Still, there is something about this man that makes my heart skip a beat. Maybe it is because of his smooth deep baritone voice and flawless chocolate skin. I cannot put my finger on it, but there is something about that man. My mind continues to return to thoughts of Malcolm for the next hour while I wait on the noon hour to arrive. I take a few minutes to freshen up in the mirror. I smooth my hair back, and I think, "Maybe it's his incredible physique that has my hormones in an uproar."

Malcolm is standing in the lobby near one of the revolving doors. He looks completely GQ with his dark six foot-five inch self in a dark suit. His jewelry is "blinging", not too much, but just right. He smiles when our eyes meet and my heart flutters. I play it cool and remind myself not to switch too hard as I approach him.

"Well good afternoon Mr. Prince," I say. In case anyone I

know is listening, I want them to know this lunch is just business, although myself I am not sure it is. Malcolm leads me to the door and escorts me to the taxicab waiting outside. We make pleasant conversation on the way to the restaurant. Malcolm sits close enough to me to make me feel uncomfortable. I scoot away from him and I manage to wedge my hips against the door of the taxicab.

We finally arrive to the small, quaint restaurant. My left hip is sore from pushing against the cab door the entire ride. We walk in the restaurant and I stand blind for several seconds. The place is extremely dim and decorated old Victorian style. There are lace table clothes, candles and real china on the tables. I wonder why he has chosen to bring me to such a formal setting. This is certainly above and beyond the type of lunch I share with most co-workers. If I did not know any better I could swear I just saw the hostess wink at Malcolm as if asking, "Sir, would you like your usual table?" I follow the hostess to the table. Malcolm is trailing behind me and I know he is looking at my behind, because I can feel it getting hot. Malcolm holds out the chair for me and after being seated himself, he promptly orders two glasses of wine. I never have alcohol at lunch, but I do not have the heart to refuse him. I take my time viewing the menu in the dim light. I sip on the wine, as I remind myself not to consume the full glass. Malcolm makes a few entrée suggestions. He has obviously been here several times.

While we wait for our order to be served, Malcolm tells me he played professional football in Indianapolis for four years before he came to work for JDL. I try to act surprised, as if I could not tell from looking at his physique. During his playing years he met his wife (his white wife) and they had three children. I try to impress him by throwing out a couple of the names of the other professional football players William has introduced me to over the years, Derrick Matthews, Al Homes, and Blaine Jarrod. Malcolm knew all the names I mentioned. We talk for several minutes about those professional football players. We both laugh and smile. Malcolm flirts with me shamelessly and I cannot resist letting him. Before I know it, I have emptied the entire glass of wine.

Chapter 9

Malcolm

I *have my sights set on the woman who is to become the next CEO of JDL. Victoria Jackson is a young, vibrant, intelligent, and sexy woman. The woman is built like a brick house and I intend to conquer her. She may be a little smarter and ambitious than some of the women I typically go for, but she is still just a woman. All women are easy. They love attention and cannot resist the pursuit of Malcolm "The Prince". That is what they used to call me when I was a professional football player in Indianapolis. Many of the fellas still refer to me as "The Prince".*

There is not a woman alive who has not had dreams of being swept off her feet by a handsome prince and living happily ever after. So it is easy for me. I play the role. I have the looks and the money. I wine and dine them. All of them, single, married, divorced, white, black, Asian, or Latino. It does not matter. I still have it going on.

Just like in my college days as a star athlete. I had women coming out of the woodwork. The women were really something back then. All of them had nice tight bodies in their late teens and early twenties. It was really hard to go wrong on a college campus. I would play two or three women on opposite ends of the campus. I would have another one or two ladies off campus. I always had a home cooked meal, someone to do my laundry and homework. I would even have another few in my hometown of Gary, Indiana, writing me, sending me money, and waiting for me to come home. The best I had in my college days were "the twins".

The twins were two identical sisters from Chicago. They were absolute knockouts. They each stood about five feet ten inches, had long straight black hair and curves in all the right places. They could have been professional models if they wanted to. Instead, they were two cheerleaders who had a special knack for getting the male fans all stirred up. The girls jumping around in tight sweaters and short skirts really had the guys all heated up before the game even started. It was rumored that "the twins" lived in a one-bedroom apartment with a king size bed for entertaining guests! During my junior year, I had an exceptionally good game. A couple of my teammates took me out for a celebration and the twins were there. The girls took me back to their place and that is when I came to realize the rumors were true. It was freak show up in there!

As good as those days were, they were only a warm up to my days in the NFL. Now my NFL days were wild! The women were breaking into the hotel rooms and would be waiting for us butt naked in the bed. The whole club scene back then was off the hook. Women from all walks of life would give you a lap dance right there in the VIP lounge. They were really throwing it out there for any one of us in a blue and white jersey. Now those were the days. A knee injury put me out of the game.

That is when I met Candy and married her for the hell of it. Candy was a knockout stripper with blonde hair, blue eyes, and a millionaire oil tycoon father in Texas. Candy wasn't stripping for the money; she was stripping to piss off her old man. I loved that rebellious spirit in Candy back then. In the beginning I tried to be faithful. But after the first baby, Candy's figure went from "knockout" to "no way". She ballooned from an hourglass figure to a two-liter. At that point, I removed Candy's practice pole from our bedroom. After baby number three, I rarely came home at all. It is not that I do not love my children. I love my children and I am a good father to them. I simply will not tolerate Candy's constant nagging. I do not have to account to her my every whereabout or share with her how I spend my money. Her checks from her millionaire father take care of the household bills and the kids. Candy does not have to get up every morning and go out and earn her pay. All she had to do *was be born. Candy left me no other choice but to go out and get what I desire. I cannot live without the love and affection of a beautiful woman. I still have game and I still have other women wanting me.*

In fact, I have plenty of other women wanting me. I had a really hot Latin intern on the nineteenth floor this past summer. I was getting up early every other morning to rendezvous with her in her office, before the early morning employees came in. Once, I was caught by Victoria leaving the nineteenth floor before 7:30 am. I am glad Victoria did not have time to talk to me that morning. I almost could not look in her in the eye after I had done what I did with that twenty-one year old hard body. School started up for the fall semester and my little intern sex toy went back to school.

Now I plan on making Victoria Jackson my number one pursuit. A woman in her position, as CEO of JDL, can be a big help to me in more ways than one. I have plans for Victoria Jackson. While I give her the love and attention that she is missing from her man at home, she can help me get my business venture started.

Chapter 10

Victoria

I work late into the evening. My lunch with Malcolm was nearly two hours long and now I am very far behind on a project. I work at a frantic pace to catch up on my project of the day. I read and reply to several email messages. Also, I do three hours of research on a new product for a business meeting tomorrow. I have to be ahead of the game. There is nothing worse than being unprepared for an important meeting. Besides, I like to make all the other Senior Executives look like peons. When the CEO asks questions in the meeting tomorrow, I want to be the one with all the answers. William is also working late at the firm, so I am not missing anything at home.

Exhaustion sets in after several hours of working my fingers to the bone. My head begins to nod and my eyelids are heavy. I try to shake it off, and blink my eyes several times, but it is no use, I fall asleep right there at my desk. I dream. I dream I am seventeen years old. It is the same dream. The same bad dream, I have had several dozen times. I see my baby brother being taken away by the police. I am helpless. There is nothing I can do to stop them, but I am just as guilty as he. I wake up at my desk in a cold sweat.

It takes me a few seconds to gather my bearings and realize I am sitting in my office on the nineteenth floor of JDL. I use a tissue to wipe away the perspiration. My heartbeat starts to slow down. "I don't have time for this nonsense," I tell myself. I feel somewhat foolish. Falling asleep at my desk and then having that stupid nightmare again. I begin to stuff the contents on my desk into my briefcase. It is eight o'clock pm and there are no other office lights on. The building emergency lights stay on in the hallways of the building and it is a good thing for me. Once I close my office door I can hardly see inside my purse to retrieve my keys to lock the door. I cannot find them. Suddenly, it comes over me like a ton of bricks. I try to resist it, but I cannot. It consumes me into a heavy darkness. I cannot catch my breath. I am down on the floor. I cannot utter a word and I cannot move. This time I see stars.

****

"David Tray found you and dialed 911. Luckily he was working late last night," William says. He is standing over my hospital bed. "They're going to keep you here over night for observation."

"Crap," I think to myself. Even in my current state of helplessness, I refuse to stay in this hospital. I try to sit up only to discover that I am hooked to an IV.

William sees my effort and shakes his head. "You're not going anywhere, Vic," he says sternly.

"When did he get so much bass in his voice," I ask myself? I frown or at least I think I do and I sit back and get comfortable. I am a strong black woman, but I am not about to take this IV out of my own arm. I just sit back and try to enjoy the ride. The ride lasts for two days.

A nurse comes in while William is sitting by my side. She asks me about my activities over the last forty-eight hours. For some reason, I do not know why, I skip over the fact that I ate lunch with Malcolm Prince. Instead I just say I had lunch with a co-worker. I feel a little bad about this little white lie. Another woman enters the room next. I assume she is another nurse, but I am wrong. She is an Employee Assistance Representative from my company. She is here to talk to me about my two panic attacks. William's eyes widen. The Employee Assistance Representative said she also recommends mental health therapy. She hands me a business card with the name Deborah L. Smith, Psychologist, and gives me instructions to follow up with a call to Dr. Smith's office to make an appointment. The rep insists I have a mental health evaluation following my panic attack on the job. I adamantly refuse to see a "shrink" and the EAP rep adamantly refuses to allow me to return to work until I submit to an evaluation with the Ph.D. I thought William would "lawyer up" and come running to my defense. Instead, William digs in his heels and agrees with my conspirators.

Before I am discharged from the hospital, William goes so far as to set the appointment for me for Friday. I do not care. I am still not going.

****

Friday evening after work, William and I meet for dinner at a fish joint on the corner of 38th Street and Keystone Avenue. You cannot get decent soul food in Carmel, where we live. We have to come to the inner city. William orders a catfish dinner with macaroni and cheese and greens. I order a perch dinner with fried okra and sweet potatoes. We both have the very sweet raspberry ice tea. We sit down at a table near the window in order to get away from the heat escaping from the kitchen. There are only six tables in the tiny room. All of them have red and white-checkered sticky plastic table clothes.

William asks how my day has gone. There is not much to share with him besides the usual drama. I try to drag it out as long as I can. "Maxine was completely outrageous today. She had on a red dress two sizes too small and you know she's a healthy woman. She was spilling out the top of the dress and I had to tell her about her old self. She really needs to dress more conservative; you know she is a grandmother. I offered to go shopping with her, but she insists on going to Lafayette Square Mall and you know how I hate the west side…"

William is not swayed, so he asks, "Baby, were you able to make the appointment with Dr. Smith?"

"No I did not. You made the appointment without consulting my calendar first. I cleared an entire afternoon in two weeks, so I have rescheduled the appointment for then."

William smiles and squeezes my hand. He bends over and

kisses me on the forehead; I hate it when he does that. I quickly change the subject. William begins talking about his day at the firm, but my mind drifts.

I sit and wonder how my mom and dad are getting along in their retirement in Ohio. I would not dare pick up the telephone and call them to find out.I wonder what kind of place the old house is in now that all of us kids are grown and gone. I never returned home after leaving for college when I was just seventeen years old. Like most other families, we had our good times and our bad times. Somehow, my bad times seemed to be the worst of the worst times. When the pain became unbearable, I left and I never looked back.

The old house was in a middle-class neighborhood. All the houses were made just alike—same color, same style, all too close together and ours too small for a family of eight. I remember things always being such a mess. It seemed clothes, dishes, and junk were everywhere. Daddy worked all day at the bank and mother was a housewife. She was home all day and the house was still jacked up. She sat around all day in hair rollers and a house robe watching soap operas. Our house was so pitiful and so embarrassing. My five brothers did not mind the mess, but I hated the condition of our home. We had the only house with more dirt than grass in the front yard. Mostly because "the boys" always had a football game going on in the yard or were driving their cars across the lawn.

It was really something growing up in that house with five older brothers—"the boys". We rarely called "the boys" by name. They were always referred to as "the boys" or "one of the boys". "The boys" were always getting into something. They fought the other kids at school, they fought all the neighborhood kids, and even fought each other at home. I could not say how many times they punched holes in walls, broke furniture, and broke at least one bone in their bodies weekly. They each had at least one extremity in a cast or a bandage on their forehead at all times. I remember when two of "the boys" got a hold of me when I was about five years old and decided they would stretch me like a rubber band. They each took an arm and started pulling! Those fools pulled my arms right out of the sockets! Our mother had to take me to the hospital. Daddy did something to them so bad for that incident none of "the boys" ever laid another hand on me!

Still, it was hard growing up in the shadow of "the boys" at times. I was the little sister of the "neighborhood hellions". In school, the teach-

ers would always expect me to behave the same as them until they got to know me. Do not take me the wrong way; "the boys" were smart. They were building bombs as kids long before the details came out on the Internet!

I hated being the baby sister of "the boys" during my teen years. They made it impossible for me to even think about getting a date. In fact, I never actually dated or had a boyfriend as a teenager. Only a few of the local boys were even brave enough to give me a second look. I was actually sweet sixteen and had never been kissed.

On the other hand, "the boys" had girls coming out of the woodwork! Their popularity on the football field and basketball court yielded numerous fans. Girls would buddy up to me to try to get close to one and sometimes more than one of "the boys". That started my lifetime of never having any true friends to call my own. Anyway, I never could keep up with which "one of the boys" was dating who. Girls came in and out of our house at all times of the day and night. Daddy should have put in a revolving door.

My only sanctuary in that house was my bedroom. I had the room all to myself since I was the only girl. When I became a pre-teen my Aunt Gail decorated my room in the fashion fit for a young lady. Daddy painted the walls lavender and laid the lavender and white carpet in my bedroom. Aunt Gail took me to the department store and bought me a white day bed. "The boys" called my bedroom "the purple puke room". I spent most of my time at home in my bedroom. When I turned fourteen and entered high school, Aunt Gail had a private telephone line installed in my bedroom and even paid the bill each month. That's when I knew I had it going on! I had to fight tooth and nail to keep those brothers of mine out of my bedroom and off my telephone. I charged them a quarter to use my phone. I have always been a shrewd businesswoman.

Now I can look back on those times and laugh. For the most part, most of my childhood was full of normal trials and tribulations. That is until things fell apart for me. I lost Aunt Gail before the start of my senior year. She was my everything. She was the youngest of my mother's sisters. She was beautiful and intelligent. Aunt Gail was an independent woman with a mind of her own. She had a fabulous career as a flight attendant. I always thought she was pretty enough to be a model. She was out of town about half of the time and the other half she spent with me. I spent so much time with Aunt Gail growing up some people thought I was her *daughter. There were lots of times, I wish I had been born Aunt Gail's child. My own mother never showered me with the love and affection Aunt Gail showed me. Mother just did not seem to have time or energy for me. It was so devastating when I lost Aunt Gail to breast cancer. I thought my whole world had fallen apart. Daddy was there for me emotionally after that. He really helped me to pick up the pieces of my broken heart. We were stuck together like glue, until he betrayed me.*

Chapter 11

Victoria

Saturday the maid service sends three candidates to interview for Maria's replacement. Although the maid service has already completed their interview process and criminal history check, my selection process is much more in depth. William busies himself in the study preparing a brief for Monday. He actually locks himself in the room and asks not to be disturbed. He is still a little ticked off over me firing Maria.

The first candidate arrives, Esther. Esther is a nearly eighty-year-old African-American great-grandmother. Esther comes complete with a crooked wig and an ancient polyester plaid ensemble. Her wig barely survives the two city buses it takes to get her here. Esther takes nearly thirty minutes to climb the stairs to the front door. She is so out of breath by the time she enters the house, she requires another thirty minutes to catch her breath before we can begin the interview. She is as sweet as pie with her southern drawl and her "baby" this and "baby" that in every sentence. Still, she would have to work around the clock at her pace to clean to my standards. I rush Esther out the door as fast as her two feet will carry her.

Then there is Helena, the young hot Latin American in her mid-twenties. Helena is brought to our house by a young Latin American male. He is driving a pimped out older model glossy purple car with a green trim. The bass coming from the Latin rap music on his radio is so loud, I can feel the vibration inside the house. I hold my breath and hope my neighbors are not at home to see this spectacle. Helena comes equipped with low rider jeans, a belly shirt and a tongue piercing. She flips her dark brown, waist length hair every time she answers a question. Helena wears fire engine red lipstick smeared across her face, black eyeliner and mascara that had to be applied with a paint brush and six inch claws that she tries to pass off as fingernails. Helena is ushered out the door faster than the speed of light.

Finally, there is Martha, the Caucasian homemaker. Martha arrives in a dusty pick up truck, which I am afraid will die in the driveway, but somehow it manages to hold on. Martha has dirty dishwater blonde hair and looks ten years older than the chronological age of forty years indicated on her application. She promptly announces she has never been on the inside of a home larger than her "mama's double wide trailer". Martha spends most of the time on the tour of our home asking, "What's this?" and "What's that?" I exhaust myself answering Martha's questions like she is a two-year old. Martha may be a bit high maintenance, but I am desperate to find someone to clean my house, so I hire Martha.

William reappears from the study just in time to be introduced to Martha. He is cordial to her, but I can tell he is still harboring resentment about Maria. When Martha says she can start Monday, William's spirits raise. He should be excited about getting a home cooked meal again, because he hasn't had one since I fired Maria. The thought of not running out of clean underwear again probably thrills him too.

Sunday morning Monique Robinson calls to invite me to attend church with her. I see her number light up on the caller ID and I do not answer the line. William is at the country club playing his usual course of golf and I am already two hours into my four-hour research project for Monday's meeting.

****

Monday I am on fire in the meeting. I think I actually see smoke coming off my behind. I make the other Senior Executives look like kindergartners. I show up at the meeting completely prepared with a wealth of knowledge and a twenty-minute power point presentation. The others may as well have shown up with crayons. They all sit idly by as I dazzle Bernard Rich. Even Malcolm Prince is sitting alongside the others with his mouth wide open holding his pitiful little Starbucks cup. A few of the others start to sweat as I put them to shame. I see a couple of them wipe their brow with a handkerchief and I notice a top lip tremble when I hit them with the power point presentation. I see Bernard Rich lean further back in his chair the more I talk. He begins to rub his fat belly, as if he knows my information is money in the bank and he is already preparing himself for a steak dinner.

The only attempt at preparedness comes from David Tray. He passes out a two-page handout. Lucky for him, his ideas piggyback on mine. Even his weak display gets the attention of the other Senior Execs. Still, he needs to upgrade to the technology of the twenty-first century. The man doesn't even know how to operate the fax machine. It is so easy to outshine this dull group of "wanna be" CEOs. They do not have the drive and determination that I have to reach the top. They only occasionally go the extra mile. I go the extra mile at every opportunity.

This time after the meeting Bernard Rich comes to my office personally. He sits across from my desk. His eyes rest on the wedding picture of William and I in the silver heart shaped frame on the credenza behind my desk. He glances quickly at the glamour shot photo of Max she gave me for Christmas a few years ago.

"What can I do for you Mr. Rich?"

"Jackson, you continue to do an excellent job here for JDL. Just between the two of us, I would like for you to know, I will be recommending you to replace me as CEO of JDL to the Board of Directors. I would like for you to think about slowing down for the next few months. Take long lunches, cut out the late nights and take a few weeks off to rest up. You'll need your strength at the beginning of the year when you assume your new position."

I stand up smiling broadly and I shake Bernard Rich's hand. I thank him for his recommendation and I assure him I will keep his decision in confidence until an official announcement is made. Bernard Rich winks at me on his way out of my office.

When he closes the door, I jump up and I am on my feet doing the happy dance! Of all days for Max not to show for work! I cannot tell any of the other Senior Executives in the office what is going on. I pick up the telephone and dial William's office number.

"Crane and Associates, may I help you?"

"Yes, William Jackson, please."

"May I ask who's calling?"

"Yes, his wife, Mrs. Jackson."

"One moment, ma'am."

I hear two clicks and William is on the line.

"Hey Vic what's going on?"

"William I have fabulous news!"

"What is it?"

"Bernard Rich just came into my office and told me privately he will be recommending me to replace him as CEO!"

"I knew it ! That's fantastic! Didn't I say you had the position in the bag?"

"Yes you did. You were right again sweetheart. How about a little celebration tonight?"

"I would love to, but I can't tonight. I have a dinner meeting with a few of the partners and a prospective client. Why don't you join us instead?"

"That's not exactly what I had in mind as far as a celebration. I'll call Monique and see if she's up to it."

I complete my call with William. I am still on cloud nine. I dial Monique's home number and she answers on the second ring.

"Hey Victoria. I was just heading out the door. Let me call you from my cell when I get to the car."

Two minutes later my private line rings and I pick it up since I am flying solo without Max here today. Monique and I get right down to business.

"I hope you are in the mood for good news! Guess who is going to become the next CEO of JDL?"

"Congratulations Victoria!"

We both yell into our phones like high school girls!

"Are you up for a little celebration?"

"Oh no! Phillip and I have tickets to a concert tonight. I'm sorry, girlfriend."

"Honey, don't worry about it. Hey, call me back when you get home from the concert tonight."

"OK. You go out tonight and have a good time for me too."

"I will. See ya."

"Bye girl."

It is times like this, I wish I had girlfriends to share in my joy.

Chapter 12

David

*T*he minute I received the news Bernard Rich announced his retirement to the Board of Directors, I knew I had to make my move. Immediately, I picked up the telephone to call my wife's first cousin, Howard. Howard sits on the Board of Directors of JDL and gives me inside information on what is going on at his level. Howard said my name has been mentioned in some circles and Victoria Jackson's name has been mentioned in others. Howard thinks if I can get some dirt on Jackson, I can persuade Bernard Rich to recommend me to become the next CEO of JDL.

I already know I am running a distant second to Victoria Jackson, but the race is not over yet. I have been a dedicated employee with JDL for twenty-five years. I started out in the mailroom as a college student and now I am the second best Senior Executive. My pace has been steady and progressive over the course of my career. I work late, go the extra mile, and I am a committed professional. I have struggled over the past five years as I have witnessed Victoria Jackson surpass my efforts. If I knew we were down to the wire for the race for CEO I would have finished the job quickly on Jackson the evening I found her on the floor outside of her *office. I had taken off my sport coat and was going to smother the life out of her when I was interrupted by the cleaning woman. If only I had left the office one minute earlier, Jackson would be dead.*

I have earned the CEO position and I intend to get it. My wife and I have raised three children of which the last two are in college. I have been both a family man and a company man. There have been many times that I have put my family second for this company. Bernard Rich has seen my efforts and he is a fool if he does not reward me for my dedication. Jackson will crash and burn at the pace she is going. I can go for several more years until I retire. Bernard Rich has to respect my work ethic and years of servitude.

I have been casually probing into Victoria Jackson's personal life and so far my efforts have yielded nothing. I could not pry two bits of information out of Maxine Rogers, Jackson's secretary. Maxine seems to be the only one around who intimately knows Jackson. I will continue to wear down Maxine. In the meantime, I have called in some professional assistance. I have retained C&J Private Investigation Firm to look into Victoria Jackson's life. Everybody has something to hide.

Nothing will stop me from getting my name on the door of the office on the twentieth floor, "David Tray, Chief Executive Officer".

Chapter 13

Victoria

I arrive home in record time and I am feeling restless. I am anxious for a real celebration. I would love to just hop into the car and pick up two or three good friends for a night on the town. It would really feel great to go out and have some serious fun! I would love to wear something that is nowhere near conservative and dance the night away at nightclub like I use to do back in the day.

I pace the floor of the house going from room to room thinking what I should do to satisfy this urge within me. I go through my list of possibilities. There is Max, from work. Good old faithful Max. She is great in social settings. Max has a way of always putting me at ease and she knows every hot spot in town. Still, I sit and ponder for five minutes if I should call Max. Afterall she did not come in to work today. Maybe she is ill or maybe she had a family emergency.

I move on to Veronica, my next-door neighbor. William and I attended a barbecue at her house last summer. She seems to genuinely like to have a good time and is pretty down to earth. Still, I hesitate. Veronica and her husband Nick have two children. Although they have a nanny, I do not want to impose on their family time.

I pick up the telephone and dial Max's home number.

"Yes, may I help you?"

"Well, I certainly hope so. You didn't hear it from me, but Bernard Rich came into to my office today to tell me he is recommending me to replace him as CEO. "

"Why does everything happen when I'm not at work? Congratulations girl!"

"You know I thought David Tray may have beaten me out of the position."

"Uptight David Tray wouldn't know a good marketing strategy if it jumped up and slapped him in the face. Even Richie Rich is smart enough to see that. Tray is not in your league. No way, Jose!"

"Well, I didn't call you to debate. I'm calling to ask if you want to go out and celebrate?"

Max pauses and takes her time saying, "I'm offended you're calling to ask me 'if' I want to go out and celebrate. You should be asking me 'what time' I want to go out and celebrate!" Max and I explode with laughter! "I know the perfect place to celebrate."

"What time should I pick you up?"

"I'll be ready at eight."

I rush into the shower and wiggle into my most fabulous and least conservative outfit. The black and white blouse shows a little shoulder up top and the black pants hug my hips especially tight. I make up my face to look extra glamorous. I reach way into the back of my closest and pull out a shoebox with a pair of clear high heel pumps. I attempted to wear the shoes out once before, but William talked about them so bad I shoved them into the back of my closet and wore a pair of shoes he found to be more "conservative" for the occasion. Tonight is my night. I am wearing my clear pumps, I am going to have a good time! William can stay at home tonight and worry about William.

I arrive at Max's house at fifteen after eight pm. She lives in a tiny three-bedroom house on the west side of town. I think to myself, she will be able to upgrade when I get the CEO position and take her to the twentieth floor with me. She will even be able to replace the gray Camry she drives, which is often broken down and forces her to take the city bus to work.

I walk up to the front door of the white vinyl siding dwelling and ring the doorbell. I am quickly greeted by the cutest little caramel-colored girl with sparkling brown eyes. She is wearing pretty pink pajamas with little brown bears floating on clouds. Her curly black hair is coming out of the ponytail on top of her head. She smiles widely and it brightens the doorway which is absent of light. I look into the eyes of this beautiful little creature and I cannot help but to smile in return. Her smile wraps around my heart and it will not let it go. The angel looks up at me and she snaps me out of the trance she has put me in when she speaks, "Are you my Grandma's friend?"

I blink several times before answering. Still smiling I say, "Yes, I am." She immediately turns around and darts through the small living room in her bare feet and rounds the corner, leaving me standing in the open doorway.

I realize as I watch her go away that I have just heard what I hear people referring to as "the pitter-patter of little feet". How sweet the little one makes this noise sound. I ask myself if I am ready to hear this very same sound in my home and I feel very uncertain. Suddenly I feel uncomfortable. I look around and realize I am still standing in the open doorway. I feel foolish just standing here. I step inside and I close the door behind me. I am struggling to find a light switch when Max enters the room.

Max hits a switch on the wall and suddenly there is light. I see her clearly in her bright red and black outfit and her granddaughter practically attached to her leg, attempting to hide behind Max's skirt. "Sorry you got left in the dark. Dominique why didn't you turn on the light?"

Dominique is not talking. She continues to smile and shakes her head "No." Maxine invites me to have a seat, which I do. She offers me a soda while she touches up her hair with the curling iron. I decline the soda, but I reach for the TV remote instead.

As Max heads back to finish her "wig", Dominique hangs out in the corner of the room. I browse through the channels until I come onto a news program and I lean back into the sofa. Dominique is obviously not pleased with my choice. In the tiniest voice she says, "Cartoons are on channel forty." I smile and invite Dominique to come sit down next to me. She smiles and hops up on the sofa. I hand her the remote and she presses the buttons until she reaches channel forty and a cartoon appears. Then, she sits back on the sofa and gets comfortable.

I sit starring at the angel. Her caramel-colored skin is perfect, not a blemish and not a scar in sight. Her curly hair and long eyelashes remind me of William. Is this what our child would look like? Would we produce a child so beautiful, so lovely and so perfect?

Before I can complete my thought Max re-enters to the room and loudly announces she is "Ready to go"!

I stand up and ask, "Where to?"

"We should go to a hot little dinner and dance spot downtown. A few of my younger friends say it's a blast."

"Younger? What kind of crowd are you talking about?"

"Don't worry. It's a thirty-five and older crowd. That makes you barely legal to get in."

Max grabs her purse from a chair in the living room and ushers Dominique to the bedroom area.

I ask, "Who's going to watch the baby?"

"I'm not a baby", Dominique says. "I'm five years-old."

Max adds, "Her mama, Chantelle, is in the back sleeping with the new baby."

Now I really shutter. The thought of twenty year-old Chantelle asleep along with the newborn and five year-old Dominique wide awake just does not seem right. I suppose Max has done all she can. She raised her three children alone after her divorce. Chantelle, her youngest, had little Dominique in high school. Max still wanted to give Chantelle a fighting chance in life, so Max paid for a babysitter so Chantelle could attend community college. Chantelle, dropped out of college after the first year. She was pregnant with the second baby. Now Max provides food, shelter and clothing so Chantelle can do what Chantelle does best. Nothing.

Max and I head east on I-70 toward town and a night of fun.

****

We pull up to a club, which is dimly lit outside. If it were not for Max's careful guidance, I would have driven right past the place. I wonder if this place is so fantastic what they have against posting a brightly lit sign outside for the patrons.

Max and I step in like we own the place. Unfortunately it is as equally dark inside and it takes my eyes several minutes to adjust to the darkness. I try to play if off as best I can by not bumping into anything or anyone. As I reach inside my purse to pay the cover charge for both Max and I, I can feel heads turn to get a good look at us. We proceed to strut in. The men look hard and they should. Max and I both know we are looking good tonight.

Max approaches the coat-check counter to check in her wrap. I did not wear one, so I simply stand around trying to look casual. The place is nice. It has two floors with a glass staircase. All of the furnishings are black and chrome. I see an extensive bar on the first floor, a nice size dance floor where quite a few people are dancing and an ample number of tables and chairs where a lot of people are enjoying what smells like good food. Most of the good tables are already full. Max completes her transaction and we step through the sitting area and find two empty seats at the bar.

The male waiter behind the bar approaches us to take our dinner and drink order. Max promptly orders a dry martini, shaken, not stirred and an appetizer sampler. I personally would not know if the waiter cheated on her order or not and decided to shake the Martini, but Max is an old pro in these matters. I order a Long Island iced tea and an appetizer sampler also. Max and I take a few minutes to check out the men trying to check us out. Max points out a few familiar faces and even does her queen wave to a few of her male admirers.

Quickly we waste no time getting to the competition. Just because an outfit comes in your size does not mean you should wear it out in public. We promptly get down to the business of deciding who is right for their outfit and who is wrong. The waiter returns with our drinks first and then comes back with the samplers. I reach into my purse to pay for the drinks. Max is all too willing to let me, she does not budge, but I am cut short. A strong hand touches my shoulder, reaches over me and drops a one hundred-dollar bill on the counter. I look up and see Al Homes, one of the professional football player types William plays golf with on Sundays. In a smooth deep voice Al says, "Please allow me."

I try to find something to say in return, "Oh, thank you. Umm...it's so nice to see you again."

"I haven't seen you and William out in a while. Where is he?"

"William isn't here. He's working late tonight."

"Well in that case, may I have this dance?" Al gestures toward the dance floor.

"Well absolutely," I say to the handsome Al Homes.

Max grabs my purse and jabs me jokingly in the behind with it as I maneuver off the barstool. "Thanks for the drink", she says, "It's so nice to know chivalry isn't dead."

"Anytime," replies Al.

I get out on the dance floor and, for the first song, I feel ill at ease. It has been a long time since I have danced at something other than a formal affair. My hips start swaying with the beat of the music and the rest of my body follows the motion. Al notices and comes in a little closer; in fact, he comes in a little too close. I take a step back and continue to get my groove on for a few more songs.

Finally Al says, "So you must be the reason I haven't seen William at the golf course lately. You must have him out pretty often with the way you dance."

"Actually William and I never go out anymore," I say to Al.

"That's a shame. A pretty woman like you should be taken out and shown off."

"I agree, but what's a married woman to do?"

"You could call me sometime. I would be happy to take you out."

"Is that right?"

"Sure. Strictly as friends that is."

The fast music turns to a slow jam.

"Well Al, let me think about that for a while. I better get back to my friend now."

I head back toward the bar leaving Al Homes standing in the center of the dance floor alone. I do not waste my time looking back. The jerk better not follow me!

I reach the bar and Max is there, guarding my barstool. However, she does not break conversation with her gentleman suitor sitting on the other side of her as she slides me my untouched drink. I gulp down half of the liquid quickly because I am hot and a little agitated by Al. Max introduces me to Joe, a handsome guy about my age and about twenty years younger than Max.

I sit and groove for a few minutes, swaying to the music and watching the other couples do their thing on the dance floor. I finish my drink and nibble on the appetizer sampler. Eventually, I order another drink. The waiter does not take my money indicating that Al's money is still covering the tab. I do not see Al anywhere and I am relieved. He golfs with my husband most Sundays and expects to step to me on the side. He better think again. I tire of listening to Joe try to lay down his rap on Max. I motion to Max toward the restroom and she nodes in approval.

I need relief in the worst way after consuming two Long Island Ice Teas. I make my way through the crowd. I imagine the club cannot fit one more body inside. The place has to be jammed to capacity by this time. I get to the restroom. I complete my business, refresh my lipstick and run a comb through my wig. I walk out feeling refreshed after experiencing a little air conditioning in the restroom. On my way back to my seat, I see Malcolm Prince. He is sitting directly in my path back to the bar. I cannot avoid him if I want to and I do want to. He looks up innocently; right away, I know he must have seen me going by on my way to the restroom.

Malcolm stops me cold at the table where he is sitting with two other men and a woman. Malcolm reaches up and takes my hand and holds it tightly. He stands and extends his arm round my waist, holding on very tightly. I am taken a little off guard, but I try to play it cool, like this sort of thing happens to me everyday.

I look down at him and smile. "Hello Malcolm. What a pleasant surprise seeing you here."

"Hello Victoria. It's so nice to see you too."

Malcolm stands and introduces me to the three people at his table and they all nod and smile. Malcolm asks me who I am here with and I tell him Max. Wrong answer. He insists on saying hello to her. I lead the way to our spot at the bar. Max is still there with Joe. Joe seems to have made some progress on his rap, because Max is smiling now. Malcolm walks up and takes Max's hand, lifts it to his lips and kisses her like she is some kind of royalty. Max blushes. Next Malcolm turns to Joe and gives him the black man's official half handshake and half hug greeting. Malcolm and Joe exchange pleasantries. "Great. The gang's all here."

Max jumps up and says, "Good. Now that I know my girl is in good hands, you two sit down and hold our seats while Joe and I go out on the dance floor." If looks could kill, Max would be dead. I shoot her a look that is so fierce I can see she gives her plan a second thought. Unfortunately, Joe is pulling her by the arm towards the dance floor now, so it is too late.

I sit for several minutes chatting with Malcolm. We have to sit close, so we can hear each other over the loud music. He buys me another drink; this makes the third one. I cannot blame it all on the alcohol, but after awhile talking to Malcolm does not seem so bad. In fact, by the time Max returns and announces she is leaving with Joe, I sit and talk to Malcolm for several more songs.

By this time it is nearly one a.m. I tell Malcolm I really must be going now. He is quite the gentleman and insists on walking me to my car. We reach my car and continue to talk. We are still so in depth into our conversation I offer Malcolm a seat inside to get out of the cool night air. Malcolm obliges. We talk for a few more minutes and then it happens. Malcolm leans forward and kisses me passionately and deeply on the lips. I do not resist. Instead, I lean in further.

Chapter 14

Constance/C&J Private Investigation Firm

I *magine the luck. My business partner Joe and I just closed a case regarding JDL the Fortune 500 marketing firm a few months ago. Helen Rich, the CEO's wife retained our private investigative services to look into a suspected relationship between her husband, Bernard Rich and his secretary. The case was easy. Pretty open and shut actually. We followed Bernard Rich and his secretary for just a few weeks. We gained entrance to the secretary's condo undetected and set up surveillance cameras. The cameras captured some pretty incriminating photos. We handed the photos over to Mrs. Rich and collected our handsome fee. Mrs. Rich paid us a hefty bonus for proof of the secretary's pregnancy too. Soon after, the news of Bernard Rich's retirement made the Indianapolis Star newspaper.*

Last week, David Tray, a Senior Executive at JDL, retained our services. He is obviously in competition to become the next CEO of JDL. He wants us to look into another employee's background, Victoria Jackson. This Jackson woman is supposed to be some kind of bitch on wheels,

*according to Tray. We are to conduct a thorough background investigation
on her and follow her around to see what dirt we come up with. He even
wants us to follow her husband for leads. He suggested we try to get close
to the nineteenth floor receptionist at JDL, Maxine Rogers. He explained
Rogers is the only employee at JDL close enough to Jackson to have any
pertinent information on her. David Tray is sparing no expense. He does
not want us to stop until we come up with something.*

*My partner Joe and I jumped right on the case. We followed Jack-
son and Rogers this week to a nightclub. Joe managed to get Rogers
wrapped around his finger in one night. Joe is one smooth talker. If it were
not for our business relationship, I could really go for a man like Joe. It is
not hard to imagine a woman falling hard for him. Perhaps I am a little
biased when it comes to Joe. Joe has been the only man I have had any
type of relationship with in the last four years. Joe and I started up the
business together and there has been little time for anything besides work.*

*Anyway, while Joe worked the Rogers angle that evening at the
nightclub, I sat in the car drinking stale coffee waiting for Jackson to leave
the nightclub. After one am she came out into the parking lot with a tall,
dark and handsome brother. It is just not fair. She already has a handsome and wealthy husband at home. I should know. I followed him for
the past two days. When Jackson and the mystery man climbed into her
car that night, I had the camera in position. When the two leaned in and
kissed, I clicked the camera, but the batteries were dead. I did not get the
shot, but there will be a next time. When it comes to matters like this,
there is always a next time.*

*The last few days we have made little progress in this case. We
have completed the customary national criminal history investigation
and employment history confirmation. We are waiting on feedback from
a connection with the Cincinnati Police Department for information on
Jackson's family background. So far the woman is clean. The bachelor's
and master's degrees on her resume have been confirmed to be authentic,
she has never been arrested and she does not have a drug problem. The
woman does not have anything more than a slew of speeding tickets on
her record. Still, there is the matter of the handsome mystery man from the
nightclub. Joe has a date with Rogers tonight, so I am sure he can get that
bit of information out of her. Maybe there was really something to that
kiss between Jackson and the mystery man. If so, we can follow up on that
angle and see how it plays out. Nonetheless, we will keep digging. Every-*

one is either doing dirt or has skeletons in their closet. *If we keep digging, we will find something. We always do.*

Once we nail this case, this will prove to be another feather in our cap, boosting our notoriety. C& J Private Investigation Firm is starting to make a name for ourselves in Indianapolis. Who would have thought Constance Mallory from Muncie, Indiana would turn out to be a big time private investigator. Certainly, not anyone who knew the Constance Mallory who grew up on the wrong side of the tracks in Muncie. Well, this girl has made it out. Now I am bound and determined to make a name for myself. This case may be just what I need; correction, it may be just what Joe and I need to put us on top.

Chapter 15

Victoria

The late October air has cooled the temperature outside, but things are still heated at JDL. Either I am a little paranoid or David Tray is on me like white on rice. The man seems to be watching my every move and he is not trying to hide it. Max said Tray has been asking her about me. Thank goodness Max is my girl and has not told him anything. It is not that I have anything to hide, because I do not. Still, I have never felt such pressure in my life. I do not like Tray lurking around every corner, waiting for me to make a mistake. I intend to continue to do what I have been doing, which is just be myself.

Max enters the office, interrupting my thoughts, and closes the door behind her. She is very brightly dressed again today in a lime green outfit with matching lime green shoes. She has a huge playful grin on her face, so I know whatever it is she has to share with me is going to be good. She plops down in one of the chairs across from my desk.

"Hey Max. What's going on?"

"Look, Joe and I are going out tonight to the new seafood

restaurant in Castleton, why don't you and William join us?"

"Max, you know William's routine. He's working late tonight as usual. Since I have slowed down my pace at work these past few weeks I've been a lonely woman. I go home to an empty house. The bed is empty when I get in it. When I awake in the morning, William is still asleep."

"From the expression on your face it looks like he hasn't even had time for a little loving," Max giggles.

"Max, don't laugh. You know me like a book. William and I have had virtually no time together lately. It would not be fair for me to complain, because I have been guilty of the same workaholic routine our entire marriage."

"Why don't you come out with me and Joe tonight?"

"No thanks. I don't care to be a third wheel. You and Joe go out tonight and have a great time. The two of you are getting pretty close aren't you?"

"Well, I don't want to brag, but yes we are. What more can I say? Joe is the perfect man. He's kind, generous, smart, and a wonderful lover," Max says with a huge grin on her face.

"Max, don't tell me you've slept with that man already!"

"Don't be such a prude. You would think you're the fifty-three year old and I am the thirty-five year old. Loosen up."

"Max it's not that I'm a prude. Lord knows I wasn't a virgin when I married William, but I didn't sleep with every man I met either."

"Joe and I are two single, young, and healthy people. We enjoy each other's company and we are having a wonderful time together. I don't want a wedding ring from Joe. I've been there, done that and got the t-shirt!"

"Max I'm not trying to judge you and I'm not trying to act like your mother, but I'm worried about you getting your feelings hurt again. I care about you. You're my girl."

"If it makes you feel any better, we're having safe sex. I don't intend to go home with something that I can't get rid of. Besides I'm too old to have any more babies. So, relax and don't you worry about me. I'm a grown woman."

"Max, I know you're a grown woman. It's just that you're important to me."

Max stands up and walks around the desk. She spreads her arms and gives me a big hug. "Girlfriend why don't you take some time off like Richie Rich suggested. Get rested up before the holidays and come back ready to start your new position."

"Max, I'm seriously thinking about it. Maybe I need to go off for a while and get my groove back, but right now William's schedule is too busy for him to get away." The thought brings a smile to my lifeless face.

"Hold up, wait a minute. If my fifty-three years have taught me anything, they have taught me not to wait on a man to have a good time. I spent eighteen years in a lifeless marriage and I learned that lesson well. Find one of your bourgeois girlfriends and run off to Jamaica or one of those other tropical places."

Max heads toward the door. Before she opens it she turns around and says, "You know you're my girl too and I worry about you sometimes."

"Thanks Max."

I sit for several minutes just thinking about what I would do if I took some time off now. I do not have any girlfriends to jump on a plane and go off for a while to relax and take the time to find myself. I do not think I could really have a good time if I go on vacation by myself. Monique would be the only friend I could even think about asking to go with me, but I would feel terrible about taking her away from Phillip and the kids. Max has already taken her two weeks of vacation leave this year. Not to mention I would have to pay Max's expenses, which I would not mind, if our finances were not so tight right now. Maybe I could ask one of my sorority sisters. It is a nice thought, but I have not kept in touch with anyone over the years.

For an instance I think about going home to Ohio for a visit. The thought leaves my mind as quickly as it entered.

****

I am on the way home from work, speeding down the interstate, when my cell phone lights up with a blocked number. I am hesitant to answer the call. Lately, I have been getting collection calls from some of the credit card companies. I take a deep breath and answer.

"Hello."

"Victoria, it's Malcolm. Have I caught you at a bad time?"

"Oh, no Malcolm you haven't. I'm just on my way home."

"I've been meaning to call you. I would love to have a chance to talk to you again. Um…and I'm feeling like I need to apologize for that kiss. In fact, that's why it has taken me so long to call."

"Malcolm there's no need to apologize. We both had a little too much to drink that night."

"Well I do not want you to think I was too forward because that was in no way my intention. I was really hoping we could get together and talk."

"That would be fine Malcolm."

"Great. Would you like to meet for dinner or just coffee this evening? Strictly as friends that is."

"Sure Malcolm. In fact, dinner would be great."

"Are you sure it won't interfere with your plans this evening with your husband?"

"Actually my husband is working late tonight, so it will not interfere at all."

"I remember you said you live on the north side of town. How does the Castleton Park Restaurant sound at seven?"

"That sounds perfect. I'll see you then."

I hang up my cell phone and I blush like a schoolgirl with a crush on the captain of the football team. I keep telling myself this is an innocent meeting of two co-workers and nothing more. I have lunch and dinner with co-workers all the time. This time is not any different. It does not matter that I am a woman and Malcolm is a man. A very tall, dark, and handsome man. A man who I kissed, long, deep, and passionately just a few weeks ago. Now I am going to dinner with this man. It just so happens that my husband is tied up with business at the firm tonight. It just so happens I have been lonely as hell these past few weeks. I sit in our big beautiful home night after night alone. I fill my evenings with aerobics, kickboxing and shopping. The excessive time to shop is killing our finances. In fact, our finances are at an all time disastrous level. I have to get a handle on things. I make a promise to myself not to spend another dime, until I sit down and refigure our budget. I will fix everything soon, but not tonight. Tonight I am meeting Malcolm for dinner at seven.

****

I arrive at the Castleton Park Restaurant at five minutes after seven. I walk inside the restaurant and ask the hostess if Mr. Prince has arrived. He has. The hostess leads me to the table. Malcolm is sitting in a warmly lit booth. He looks handsome dressed in all black. He stands to greet me and kisses me lightly on the cheek. I blush and sit down still smelling the pleasant aroma of his cologne. I notice Malcolm has taken the liberty to order two goblets of wine. Again, I tell myself not to finish the entire goblet. When the waitress comes to take our order, I order a glass of water to avoid the wine.

Malcolm and I talk casually all night. We talk about the last time we saw each other outside of work at the dinner club. We both talk about how we do not get out much with our spouses. We talk about spending a great deal of effort on our careers. Malcolm brings up the rumors at JDL about me becoming the next CEO. I try my best to dispel the rumor. Malcolm talks about his interest in starting his own marketing firm, which will cater to pro-athletes. He has a couple of interested investors and he plans to leave JDL and become an entrepreneur. I congratulate Malcolm for his courage to go out on his own.

We talk like we have known each other forever. The way William and I used to talk before our careers took over our lives. Malcolm and I enjoy a good meal and even better wine. I finish the entire goblet of wine. When our meal and dessert are complete, Malcolm offers to pay the bill. I let him. When the time comes for the night to end and us to depart, Malcolm walks me to my car once again. As we say our good-byes, Malcolm takes my hand and kisses it ever so lightly.

It is a good thing Malcolm only kissed Victoria's hand, because the both of them were totally oblivious to the camera clicking just two tables away the entire time they were together. At the new seafood restaurant two miles down the road, Max is sitting at dinner with Joe, unaware their conversation is being recorded.

Chapter 16

Malcolm

The night is still young and I just don't quite feel like going home. Candy is home with the kids tonight, so there really is no reason for me to rush home. Lately, Candy has been nagging me so much I am thinking about moving out and getting my own place. The kids can come and visit me some weekends. They are the only reason I go home at all anyway.

I wish Victoria had been more willing to take things to the next level tonight, but I can work at her pace. I can take it fast or I can take it nice and slow. It really doesn't matter as long as I eventually have my way with her.

The wine at dinner has me relaxed and ready to do something tonight. I pull out my cell phone and call one of my women on standby. Marla from JDL answers on the second ring.

"Hello."

"Hey baby, it's me. What's up tonight?"

"I hope you and me."

"Is your roommate there?"

"No, she's at her boyfriend's apartment for the night."

"Sounds like an invitation."

"Consider it one."

"I'll be there in ten minutes."

I am at least thirty minutes away from Marla's apartment on the south side of town, but I like to keep her waiting. Marla is a cute little chocolate girl with long black silky hair and a fantastic body. She works at JDL in the Accounting Department as a clerk. She is just one of my many women I have on standby at work. I already have at least one woman on every floor at JDL. There is something so addictive about women, about sex.

Marla is so eager to please. She calls me at least twice before I arrive to make sure I'm still coming. The first time she calls I let the cell phone ring and I do not bother to pick it up. I love to keep them guessing. The second time she calls I pick it up and Marla tells me all about how she is getting ready for me. She has placed royal blue silk sheets on the bed and she has on a matching royal blue teddy. She has a warm bubble bath running for me and her best fluffy towels on standby waiting to dry off every part of my body. Marla asks me to pick up a bottle of wine on my way and I am more than happy to oblige.

I drive into the parking lot of a nice upscale liquor store to get a bottle of wine for Marla and I to enjoy. As I exit my Escalade, I am approached by an attractive young Latin American female. She is wearing all red leather. The leather fits her like her skin. It is smooth over all of her curves. My weakness for Latino women must show on my face, because she walks right up to me and asks me if I want a "date". We back up and lean against the Escalade. I look around just to make sure this is legitimate and everything is cool. I notice nothing unusual as I scan the parking lot and surrounding area.

"How much?" I ask.

"How much do you wanna party?" she asks in return, leaning against my Escalade.

"How much for a blow job?"

"One hundred."

"Baby you're fine, but that's a little too steep. How about fifty?"

"Baby I promise I'll make you feel real good."

"Let me go in here and pick up a bottle of wine and I'll get back with you."

I go inside and survey the selection of wine. I make my purchase quickly. All the while, I'm thinking about the fine young thing outside waiting to make a sell. A hundred bucks is high for a regular streetwalker. I can drive to East Washington Street or the corner of 30th and College and get a blowjob for only twenty dollars. Yet this girl is fine. The red leather is kicking. Her butt is big, her waistline is slim, and Lord knows I cannot resist a woman with a wide gap between her legs. Sold!

I drive around to the back of the liquor store with the red leather hooker in the Escalade and I park. I unbutton my pants and she goes to town on me like the pro she is.

I arrive at Marla's house more than an hour after I originally called her. She opens the door with an attitude.

"What took you so long?"

"You asked me to stop and get a bottle of wine. I had to stop at two different stores to find the kind you like."

"Did it really have to take you so long? Your bath water is cold now."

"I'll chill the wine, while you run some fresh bath water."

Marla stands there in the middle of the small living room still pouting. She looks great in the royal blue teddy, but her attitude is really killing my good mood. This is exactly why I rarely hook up with black women—too much attitude. I had a wonderful dinner with Victoria tonight. I had a damn good blowjob by the hooker. Now all I want is some hot sex with Marla to top off my night, but her attitude has me tempted to walk out of the apartment and leave her standing there.

Marla finally speaks, "I bet you don't keep your wife waiting like this."

Why did she have to go there? "Didn't I tell you I'm not married!" I shout. She has me pissed off now.

"Malcolm everybody at JDL knows you're married to some rich white woman. It's not fair how you do me. You had me waiting around here for over an hour tonight. We've been kicking it for six months now and you barely even see me once a week."

"Marla come on now, not tonight. I didn't come over here to be nagged. I told you I'm divorced, but I'm not able to make the kind of commitment to you that you want right now, because of my busy schedule at JDL."

"Bullshit Malcolm! I see you come in the office every morning at nine and most days you leave before five. Today you left work at three o'clock. Its eleven o'clock and you're just now getting here. I'm tired of being last on your list. I'm not going to sit around here waiting on you to call anymore. I'm moving on with my life Malcolm."

If I wanted to be nagged to death tonight, I could have gone home to Candy. "Hey do what you want to do Marla." I turn and head to the front door.

"Fuck you Malcolm!" Marla shouts. She grabs the bottle of wine from the cocktail table and throws it at me with all of her might. The bottle bursts on the wall just to the right of the front door and the contents spill all over my suit.

"You crazy ghetto bitch! What the fuck are you doing?" By this time I am seeing red. Before I know it I have Marla on the living room floor and I am holding her with both hands by the throat and I am chocking the life out of her. Marla is trying her best to get away, but she is no match for me. Her efforts yield no results. She cannot release from my grip and her airflow is completely blocked. Marla claws at my hands with her long fake fingernails digging deep into my flesh, but I hold on. The look of shock on her face finally gets through to my conscious and I release my hold, but I feel no remorse.

Marla is gasping and trying to crawl away from me. I reach out and grab Marla by one leg and I pull her back to me. I take from Marla what I came here tonight to get.

Chapter 17

Victoria

I am having the midweek blues. It is Wednesday, hump day, and I am thinking about cutting my workday short. Today I just cannot seem to concentrate. The rumors of competition between David Tray and me for the CEO position are getting fierce. I know it would be unwise for me to let the cat out of the bag and tell them all the position is mine. Still, it is so hard keeping such a fantastic secret. I want so badly to tell them all David Tray does not have a snowball's chance in hell of getting the CEO position.

Right now I have to continue to keep my mouth shut and I have to make sure Max keeps her trap shut too. Lately, she has been so wrapped up into her new boyfriend, Joe, she talks of little else. Max is really falling hard for this guy. I cannot explain what is going on with my love life.

I cannot get my mind off of Malcolm Prince. Every bone in my body yearns to be more than friends with Malcolm. Every time he calls me my heart skips a beat. We have been meeting for lunch or dinner twice a week lately. Malcolm calls me almost every day and I look forward to his calls. It is not so much what he says, but moreso the attention. Lately, if I do not call and interrupt William at the office, some days we do not talk at all.

Deep down inside, I know I should put the breaks on this thing with Malcolm before it goes too far. Besides, what about William? The husband I see for only a few hours each week. The husband who is always working at the firm or on the golf course. What about the man I fell in love with? William used to set my heart on fire. Lately, it seems his touch barely makes a spark inside of me. Lately, he barely touches me. I thought we were a strong partnership that could withstand the test of time. What is a woman to do?

My private line rings and I answer it.

"Victoria Jackson"

"Victoria, it's Monique. Is now a good time for you?"

"Yes. Right now is a great time. I really need to talk to you girlfriend?"

"What's wrong?"

I try to reply to Monique's question, but I cannot. Tears well up in my eyes and words will not escape my mouth.

"Victoria? Are you there?"

"Yes," I manage to mutter through the tears.

"Victoria what's wrong? Can you hear me?"

"Yes, I can hear you. I need someone to talk to."

"I'm here for you Victoria. What's wrong?"

"I need to get out of this place."

"I'm at home today. I took the day off so why don't you come on over. The kids are gone to the Children's Museum with the Nanny, so we can talk uninterrupted."

"I'm on my way."

Thank God for Monique. I clean the mascara streaks off my face and head out of the office to Monique's house. Before I know it, I am sitting in Monique's modest living room while she prepares some hot tea for us to sip on. I look around at the pictures of Monique, Phillip and the children on the walls. They seem so happy. They seem to be a perfect little family. Everything seems to be so perfect and in order. Monique looks so relaxed and comfortable in her sweat suit. She does not seem to have the lines of stress on her face, like the ones that settled on my face long ago. While their home is half the size of ours, they probably are not swimming in debt. Phillip probably comes home in time for dinner every night. He owns his law practice and makes his own hours. He does not have the pressure of pleasing his partners like William does. They probably put the children to bed together, kiss them on their precious little cheeks, and retire to their bedroom for husband and wife time. I wish I had it so good.

Monique enters the room with a tray of hot tea. She serves the both of us. She takes only lemon with her tea and I take both lemon and sugar. As soon as she settles on the comfortable sofa by my side, I waste no time telling her everything. I tell her about the panic attacks. I tell her about the debt William and I have accumulated and how we just cannot seem to get from under it. I tell her about the competition for the CEO position at JDL. I hesitate, but I even tell Monique about Malcolm and the feelings he has stirred inside of me. Monique is a real friend. She does not judge me; she does not try to make me feel bad about some of the awful decisions I have made. Instead, she sits and listens. She holds my hand and helps me get through the tough parts. She hands me a tissue when I start crying halfway through my confession. When I have said all I can and I break down in uncontrollable sobs, Monique holds me in her arms like I am one of her children. She holds me and rocks me for a long time. Finally, I take a deep breath.

"What should I do?"

"The first thing you have to do is talk to William. It's only fair that he knows what's going on with you. It probably would be a good idea for you to take some time off work right now, while you're sorting through all of this."

"I can't believe what a mess things have become for me. The only one thing I'm sure about is that the CEO position is mine, if I want it. I thought this was my dream come true, but now I'm not sure if I want it any longer."

"What makes you unsure now?"

"I'm not sure if I want to become the first African-American female to hold the position of CEO for the prestige or if I truly want to make a positive difference for JDL. When I was an undergraduate student at Central College my goal was to become a successful and powerful business professional for the sole purpose of giving back to the community. That was my motivation for attending graduate school. I wanted to be the top in my field. I had dreams of bringing

other young African-Americans into the business world. I wanted to
create a business environment where other African-Americans would
not have to be ostracized. An environment where they would not
have to work harder than everyone else just to be accepted as an
equal."

"Well you can do all of those things and more, once you
become CEO."

"I don't know, Monique. It's been years since, I've really
believed in that dream. I've spent the last twelve years in Corporate
America climbing the ladder of success for my own benefit. I haven't
done a single thing to bring another minority into the corporation. I
write two checks each year; one to my Historically Black alma mater
and the other to my sorority's annual scholarship fund. I have done
nothing hands on to make a difference."

"Victoria this is your opportunity to do more. This is your
chance to put some of your creative ideas to work. It's your chance to
provide an even playing field for those coming after you. I'm not trying to tell you what to do. The decision is yours and you have to feel
good about the decision you make."

"That sounds just like the advice they gave us in the conference I attended this past summer on 'Successful Women in Business'."

"Did the conference address the dilemmas of the black female
professional?"

"Not exactly. That would've made the discussion pretty awk-
ward with me being one of only two black females out of the two
hundred participants at the conference."

"This is definitely not an issue white female professionals have
to deal with. Their glass ceiling is a single-paned glass. For black
women the glass ceiling is double-paned glass behind a reinforced
steel door."

"I'm so tired, Monique. I'm so tired of it all. I don't even know
how I really feel about anything at all. I don't know if I can make
William happy in all of this. If we do get through this financial mess,
I don't know if he'll ever be happy without us having children."

"Do you want to have children with William?"

"I don't know. I've never really let myself think about it truthfully. All I know is all of the really successful women don't have chil-

dren. Since I want to be one of those women, I thought it was only logical that I not have children either."

"You can't let other people make decisions for you."

"I know. It's almost like I'm afraid to make a decision about anything. My track record has not been so great lately. Look at what I've done with our finances. William will be so disappointed in me about the debt."

"Victoria, you shouldn't feel alone in this situation. William is your partner in your marriage and that means he is your partner in your finances. William has to take some of the responsibility for the debt the two of you have accumulated during the marriage."

"He trusted me to do the record keeping and take care of the bills."

"But he takes part in the spending Victoria, so he needs to take part in the repayment of the debt."

"I might be able to tell William about the debt and even about what is going on at JDL, but I will never be able to tell him about Malcolm."

"Victoria, you don't have to rush into everything all at once. Take your time, and really think things through. Take one step at a time. William loves you and he is devoted to you. Remember he vowed to be with you for better or for worse. Right now you are going through a tough time and I believe William will understand. I know he will understand everything."

"But Monique, I hardly ever see William. I hate to use our few precious moments together to talk about the mess I've made of things lately."

"I'm not trying to tell you what to do, but I'm trying to give you the best possible advice I can. Be honest with William. It's the only way to maintain a strong and healthy marriage."

"Monique, you're such a good friend. How did you learn to give such great advice?"

"It comes from years of watching Oprah," Monique says smiling and then we both laugh. "Over the years I've had to learn to take advice myself. Phillip and I do not have a perfect marriage. We went through a pretty rough time just a couple of years ago and Phillip wanted to separate. Honestly, I was against the separation because at the time I felt completely financially dependent on Phillip."

"Oh Monique, I had no idea."

"It was a difficult time for me. I went into counseling for about a year. During the counseling I decided to begin to work part-time with Phillip. The law office is something we have both invested our time and money in. I feel a greater since of self worth now that I am earning an income."

"Oh Monique, I'm so sorry I wasn't there for you like you have been able to be here for me now."

"There's no need to apologize. Trust me, I was not a perfect wife to Phillip when he and I were going through our difficulties and he had every right to want to leave. I'm so grateful we were able to work things out."

"I'm so grateful for a friend like you."

Chapter 18

Monique

I *have known Victoria and William since before they were married.*
I have never seen Victoria break down and show as much emotion
as she did today. Victoria is a good person at heart. Her drive and
determination to be the best in everything she does makes it difficult for
others to get to know her or to get close to her. In fact, it makes it difficult
for others to see the good in her. I have been blessed with the uncanny
ability to see past the outer shell in others. When I look at Victoria, I see
a scared little girl, running from something. Heck, the woman moves at
the speed of light in all she does. If she is not running from something, I
don't know who is.

Fortunately for Victoria, she has the love of a good man. Her mar-
riage with William is strong. I believe with all of my heart they can get
through this tough time; however, Victoria will have to be willing to
admit to herself that she is not perfect. She will have to admit she needs
William's help. She works so darn hard to be perfect. Her first priority is
to be the perfect executive. She places her perfect million-dollar home
before her perfect man. She has her priorities all screwed up.

William adores Victoria. I have always been a little jealous of the intensity of passion and adoration that William obviously feels for Victoria. My husband, Phillip, is just not the type of man who feels so passionately about his woman. When Phillip talks about me, I never see his eyes light up the way William's eyes light up when he talks about Victoria.

It is not that I am unhappy in my marriage; I am content. I would just love to have a man feel that kind of passion for me. I wonder if she even sees in him what I see in him. I wonder if she even realizes her husband is drop dead gorgeous. I have seen William in his bathing suit on the beach in Hilton Head when we vacationed together. The man literally stopped traffic! All eyes were on William. All of the women took a second look at William as he walked by. All of the men tried to stick out their chests and hold in their stomachs a little more, but none were in his league. Even my own husband, Phillip, pales in comparison to William. I could not keep my eyes off of William the entire time. His dark, thick curly hair, beautiful brown eyes, caramel-colored skin covering mounds of muscles had me hypnotized. Silly, Victoria spent half of her time, talking business on her cell phone that afternoon.

I sincerely hope Victoria gets it together in time to save her marriage. She has a good thing going with William. She needs to slow down long enough to open her eyes to the treasure she has in him. William is any woman's dream man. He is a handsome, rich lawyer, who adores his woman. The only thing the man wants is to have a couple of kids. William has been talking about starting a family since he and Victoria were newly married. I do not understand her refusal to start a family. These days a woman can have a career and a family too. Any other woman would be happy to oblige to William's desire for a family. If Victoria loses William over this relationship with some other man, she is a fool. William will not be single and alone for very long. Another woman will be happy to have him. Heck, if Victoria does not want William, I will take him in a heartbeat.

I tried to approach William last year on our vacation to Hilton Head. William was alone in the entertainment room of the house we rented watching a movie on television. Phillip and Victoria had long been asleep. I was in the kitchen preparing food for the next day. As I walked past the entertainment room, where William sat all alone looking sexy, I could not resist. I stopped in and asked him if I could get him something to drink. He politely thanked me, but said he was okay. I approached William on the sofa and allowed the bathrobe I was wearing to drop to the floor. William's focus changed from the large screen TV to the strip tease I was performing for his eyes only. William raised an eyebrow at first, but he said nothing and he did not move. Next, I slipped off my undergarments; still no reaction from William. I mounted William and began to kiss him passionately on the lips. William did not kiss me back but he let me kiss him. I felt his strong hands on my hips and then he pushed me away. I fell to the floor of the entertainment room directly in front of the big screen TV William had been starring at. He rejected me. Quietly William said, "This is a mistake." He stood up and walked out of the room, leaving me on the floor feeling like a fool. He has never said a word about it. As far as I know he never said a word to Phillip or Victoria.

Chapter 19

Victoria

After I leave Monique's house, I drive around for hours aimlessly. I have absolutely no destination. I get on the highway and I get off still with no ending point in mind. I have no sense of time and I do not even bother to look at the clock on the wood grain dashboard in my car or the diamond watch on my wrist.

I continue to drive. I am going nowhere, but I am going there fast. I am driving at high speed through intersections as if I am on a high-speed chase. No one is chasing me and I am not chasing anyone. Instead, I feel like I am running. I feel like there is something, or maybe someone, on my tail and I just cannot shake them. I just cannot go fast enough to break away from the hold that has me bound. I operate like a plane on autopilot. Like a robot, like a machine, like a thing, but not like a woman. It is like I am no longer a woman with warm blood flowing through my veins, with a heart that beats, a heart that loves, and a soul that lives.

I drive until dusk. I feel something stirring inside of me. The feeling is complete and utter exhaustion. The kind of exhaustion that you feel in your bones. The kind of exhaustion that a good night's sleep will not heal. No. This kind of exhaustion requires some serious soul searching. I need an explanation for so many things. Why? Why? Why?

I stumble onto a park on the north side of town. I turn my car into the parking lot, find a place to park and get out. I need fresh air. I need to breathe. Right now I feel like I am going a little crazy. I take in the cool autumn air and it feels so good. Autumn is my favorite season of the year. I love it when the leaves turn their beautiful rich colors. The leaves seem to fill the air with a scent all their own. Mixing that smell with hot cider and fried biscuits with apple butter from Brown County, Indiana, is just like heaven. Right now, I wish I were snuggled in William's arms in front of a warm fireplace. It would feel so good to be safe and warm in his arms.

I walk over to a metal bench. I look out across the distance at two small children playing on a swing set under the careful watch of their mother.

I take off and start walking. This time I am on foot, so I try to pay attention to where I am going so I can eventually get back to my car. I find a walking trail and I am on my way. Quickly I am passed on the trail by two joggers. I continue to walk briskly. I think about everything. Suddenly I am walking and reevaluating my entire life. All the while I am asking myself, "Where did I go wrong?" I continue to walk. Suddenly, I stop and I look around at my surroundings. Finally I look at my watch, the diamond watch.

I was so excited when William bought me the watch two years ago for Christmas. It cost more than fifty thousand dollars. It made me feel like I was sitting on top of the world when he gave it to me. Now it means nothing. In fact, it, along with numerous other pricey items, is the reason I have been driving around in a near catatonic state for the past few hours.

I have always been so attracted to things that shine and glitter. As a teenager, I developed a love for dressing in the most hip and trendy clothes. I was an eighties fly girl. I topped off my fly girl look with the latest designer jeans and gold jewelry. I wore every trendy name on the backside of my jeans. Even back then, I had to be number one. There was never anything too good for me as far as I was concerned. If it meant I had to beg, borrow, or steal, that is what I did to get the things I wanted.

Stealing is exactly what lead my baby brother to jail. Once we became teenagers, my brother and I both were attracted to designer clothes and glittery jewelry. However, we could not afford any of it. The summer before my senior year, I was determined to set myself apart from the rest of my high school classmates. My baby brother and I devised a plan to purchase a credit card from a local entrepreneur. He charged us three hundred dollars to use an American Express Card for one day.

My baby brother and I decided to use the card at the Fashion Mall in Dayton, Ohio. It was just forty-five minutes from Cincinnati and offered a much trendier selection than any of the Cincinnati malls. We could not tell our parents where we were going. Daddy had forbidden us to drive on I-75 between Cincinnati and Dayton. There had been numerous fatalities on the highway and he said that stretch of the interstate was unsafe. Needless to say, we missed numerous concerts and other events in Dayton. The only time we ever got to Dayton was when Daddy took us himself. So my baby brother and I concocted a story and told our parents we had tickets to Kings Island, so we could borrow mother's car all day.

My baby brother bought the stolen American Express Card on a Friday night. I practiced all evening signing my name like the signature on the back of the card. We got up early on Saturday morning and headed for Dayton. We drove all the way without a hitch. Not a single fender bender occurred that day, what did Daddy know anyway? We mixed into the mall crowd that busy Saturday morning with a shopping spree on our minds.

I remember feeling "high" from the experience. Anything and everything was at my disposal. I get that same "high" feeling even today when I am in the mall. I want to buy, buy, and buy until my heart is content.

My baby brother did not want us to bring too much attention to ourselves so he cautioned me to make only a single purchase at each store. In addition, he did not want us to be seen carrying more than one shopping bag each. So, when our shopping bags filled up we took turns taking the bags to the car. After several trips to the car and a stomachache from all the junk food, we were both pretty tired. The "high" I experienced earlier that day had long since worn off.

It was nearly an hour before the mall closed and my baby

brother wanted to stop and go home. I had not yet bought myself my first Coach bag so I wanted to press on. We went inside one of the major department stores and we planned to make one purchase in every department. Unfortunately, our shopping bags were full again and it was my turn to take the bags to the car. He went on without me and said he would meet me at the jewelry counter. By the time I traveled to the car and returned our shopping spree was abruptly ended.

I entered the department store in time to see my baby brother being escorted by two uniformed police officers passed the jewelry counter toward a side door. I followed at a distance. As the two uniformed officers neared the side door I could see a waiting police car, with lights flashing. My baby brother resisted the officers. He was looking around and I knew he was looking for me. I sped up my pace until I was visible to him. His eyes met mine for a brief moment. He stopped resisting and went on with the officers. I did not know what to do. I stood helplessly by as my baby brother went to jail. I continued to stand by helplessly as he served a one-year sentence for "our" misdeed.

All of the heart, pain, and fear from the incident came rushing back to me. My mind came rushing back to the present. Here I am, standing in the middle of a park. It is nearly dark. I do not hear the noises of the children who were playing earlier on the swing set. I begin to look around. It is as if I am looking through my eyes for the very first time. Everything seems so clear. I turn around and head back to my car. This time I drive slowly. I have a purpose. I know where I have to start…at the beginning.

Chapter 20

Baby Brother

I *love my sister dearly. When I talked to mother this week, I was glad to hear Victoria is finally coming home. I am excited about her coming to visit me too, but more than anything, I am grateful Victoria is finally giving herself the opportunity to work things out with our parents.*

I have always felt sorry for Victoria. She had it rough growing up in a home with five brothers. Back in those days, I was not much of a role model. I tried to lead Victoria in the right direction some of the time, but I was too busy with my own issues. I was a gay African-American teenage boy growing up in a conservative city, in a house with four rough and tough brothers. I had not come out of the closet yet, so I did not know my own role in the world yet either.

I knew then that I loved Victoria and I always would. Since we were just a year apart, early on I became Victoria's protector and confidant. As little kids we did everything together. We were like twins. When you saw one, you saw the other. We had identical red, white, and blue bicycles with silver streamers dangling from the handlebars. Daddy bought us both the masculine version of the bicentennial bikes, although

I would have preferred the feminine version. Throughout the school year, we wore identical blue jeans and plaid hand-me-down shirts from our older brothers. In the summer, we converted the blue jeans to cut off jean shorts. I cut my jean shorts about an inch and a half shorter than I cut Victoria's shorts.

As a preteen, I was the one Victoria told when she started her period. She bypassed Mother and came straight to me with the news. I went to the store with her to get her first box of sanitary napkins, halfway because I was curious about them myself. Victoria told me all of her secrets and dreams during her teenage years. She told me about her first crush. She had a major crush on the boy next door. I did not have the heart to tell her at the time, I had a crush on him too.

Over the years, Victoria developed a very close relationship with our Aunt Gail. As a child, I was a little jealous of their relationship. I loved Aunt Gail too and she was everyone's favorite Aunt. However, when Victoria left home to spend weekends with Aunt Gail, I was left alone in that house to pretend to be just another one of "the boys". I always knew that I was not like the rest of my brothers and that I was different.

When we lost Aunt Gail to breast cancer, it affected Victoria much more than the rest of us. It seemed like she lost her own will to live. That was some kind of pain and heartache for a teenage girl to withstand. I thought I was doing my little sister a favor when I bought that stolen credit card. I thought taking her on a shopping spree would lift her spirits. I thought it would help her to become whoever it is she wanted to be. Even if she just wanted to be "best dressed" in her high school yearbook. I must admit it was not all about Victoria's needs. I loved to shop just as much as she did. Fashion was everything to me back then.

I experimented with sewing a little in those days. I made Victoria's dress for her junior prom and I planned to design a fabulous ensemble for her senior prom, but suddenly I was no longer around. I royally screwed things up for Victoria and me. Just when she needed me the most, I went and got myself locked up. I should have been more careful. We had shopped all day on that stolen credit card and I should have put my foot down and insisted it was time to go home. But I never could say no to Victoria. Whatever my sister wanted, I always gave her. She just wanted to go into one more store and purchase her first Coach bag. I did not have the heart to refuse her. Like an idiot I sashayed right up to the jewelry counter and tried to cop a fat gold chain. I knew I had gone too far as soon as I did it. Those cops were all over me like a fat lady on a piece of chocolate cake. The moment I saw Victoria's eyes and the look of fear and disappointment in them, I knew I had royally screwed up.

Things only got worse for me when I was taken to jail. All of those years of questioning my sexuality and trying to figure things out for myself came to a rushing halt. The other guys in jail promptly straightened things out for me, by slapping me in the face with the cruel reality that I was a "fag" as they quickly began to call me.

Still at the tender age of eighteen, although I was still a virgin and had strong feelings for men, I was not ready for the cold reality of the street term used to refer to me. Jail offers you no closet in which to hide. There are no closets to hide your fear, your sadness, your embarrassment, or your pain. There are no closets to hide your face when you cry and your shame when you have just been beaten up and you have two black eyes. There are no closets at night to hide the men masturbating on the top bunks or the ones having sex on the bottom bunks. There are no closets to hide the tragedy of a grown man being called a "bitch", "ho", and "trick".

Despite the name-calling, I was never ashamed of the type of man I am and I held my head up high. I continued to hold my head up high during the court trial. I remained steadfast while serving the one year sentence in the county jail.

Abruptly everything changed after I killed a man in the county jail who tried to rape me. I killed him with my bare hands. I had always been strong. My brothers had been football players and I always enjoyed lifting weights with them. I was amazingly strong. I was sentenced to fifty years for Manslaughter and sent to the Ohio Department of Corrections. My first lover there named me "Peaches" and I have been known as "Peaches" ever since.

I am very comfortable in the skin I am in. I have my own family here in Prison. Many of us have been here together for a very long time. We have grown up together in this place we now call home. In addition, we help to provide one another with the much needed protection that is necessary for gay men to survive in prison. Not all gay men are promiscuous freaks. Most of us want the same thing everybody else wants. We want to be loved and accepted for who we are, we want to be in a committed relationship and we want to be left the hell alone.

NOVEMBER

Chapter 21

Victoria

I-74 has certainly changed a great deal. I am ashamed to admit I was in Cincinnati for a business conference just three years ago and I never even bothered to go see my family. I did not see my parents and not a single one of my brothers. I came into town, did my business, and got out of town just as quickly as I could. I even told William my conference was in Columbus, Ohio so I would not have to hear any negative feedback from him.

I am nearly fifty miles into my journey now—halfway there and halfway back home. As the miles fly behind me, it is harder and harder to resist the urge to turn around and go back. I press on the gas pedal and speed ahead. I move on to resolve the pain, hurt, and confusion that I started running away from eighteen years ago. The guilt is swelling up in my throat and I practically choke on it all the way there.

It is funny how time flies. The first seventeen years of my life seemed to have taken forever. The next eighteen years have flown by like the blink of an eye. It is amazing once you become consumed in your own life the world seems to close up around you. My world became a strange place. Every year there were fewer connections with my family. My letters to my baby brother have become less and less personal over the years. He stopped asking me to visit him and the family years ago. Now he sends me "updates". "Okay, here is a list of the changes in the lives of our family since the last letter I wrote you", kind of thing. If it were not for my baby brother and the occasional Christmas card and birthday card, I would be totally disconnected from my family.

My oldest brother never forgets a birthday. Like clockwork, every year I get a birthday card form him on my exact birthday, unless it happens to fall on a Sunday. It always amazes me how he does that. When we were kids he always made a big deal of everyone's birthday. He made everyone feel so special on their special day. He even went all out on Daddy's and Mother's birthdays too. He would make all of us kids chip in our pennies and buy them a birthday cake and gift from all of us. Every year Daddy and Mother would pretend to be so surprised.

My oldest brother has a heart of gold behind his rough and tough exterior. No one would know just by looking at him that he has a soft spot in his heart for birthdays. I bet my oldest brother's wife really appreciates that about him. I know he is a wonderful father to his four children. I can just see him four times a year having a huge birthday party for each of his children. I can just see him running around, enjoying himself, and having more fun than the kids.

I will never forget my first birthday after my Aunt Gail died. My oldest brother gave me the biggest birthday party I have ever had in my life. It was a surprise party and boy was I surprised. I was so surprised I wanted to run into my room and cry, but I resisted the urge. At that time I was still very sad and pretty much just wanted to be left alone. I wanted so very badly to lash out at him and everyone there. I wanted them all to see I had lost my will to live. My Aunt Gail was gone and so was my baby brother by then. I did not want a birthday party; I wanted a pity party.

In the beginning, I felt like a captive that night. It seemed I was forced to participate in the celebration of my birth. I stood numb surrounded by parents, brothers, cousins, uncles, aunts, grandparents, and neighbors. In the end I had a good time.

Going home makes me think of so many things. So many

things I have not thought about in a long time. Going home makes me afraid. I am afraid each corner I turn when I enter the city will remind me of Aunt Gail. I am afraid it will be just too painful to be back in my hometown. I am afraid the minute I smell the fragrance of the city, I will also smell the fragrance of her perfume. I am afraid when I see the skyline of the city I will hear her voice pointing out each location we were at together. I can picture Aunt Gail smiling in my mind and pointing at the Zoo, where we went every spring. There is the Ballet, where we would get dressed up and attend each summer. There is the Stadium where we went to see the football games every fall. Around every corner is a memory and around every corner is pain.

My life is a mess and her life was so perfect. She had the perfect career. She loved to travel as a flight attendant. She had the perfect husband, who supported her career choice. Even as a child, I was jealous that she was away so often. It did not seem to bother her husband. He spent his time running his own business while she was gone. In my eyes, they were the perfect couple. They had it all: two successful careers and a good marriage.

Most of all, Aunt Gail seemed so happy all of the time. Every time I saw Aunt Gail she had a smile on her face. Her smile was the kind of smile that would light up a room. The kind of smile that would make you smile in return, even if you were in a bad mood and did not feel like smiling. Her smile gave me inner peace. Her smile told me deep down inside everything was going to be all right. Her smile let me know angels are alive and walking on this earth. I had an angel in my life. That is until the cancer. It spread, but it never took away her joy and her happiness. It never took away her smile. Not even at the very end.

Eventually I accepted Aunt Gail's death and even the role I played in my baby brother's incarceration. Still I do not know if I will ever be able to accept what my father did.

Chapter 22

Daddy

I love all of my children. I love them all in a special way, as all fathers do. This week was so wonderful for me, because finally my baby girl came home. She had not been home since she left to go away for college eighteen years ago. I cannot blame her. I know I had a lot to do with her decision.

I thank the Lord that he blessed me to have six children with my wife of nearly fifty years. We raised the children as best we knew how. We certainly made a lot of mistakes. This past week with my baby girl we all had a chance to talk about some of those mistakes. We did some apologizing and some forgiving too.

It was just so good seeing her again. The picture of her that I held in my mind for so many years was the picture of a sad seventeen year-old girl. Her mother and I took her to Central College so many years ago. She looked so small, so sad, and so frail. I can still see her standing in her dorm room full of luggage, boxes, and books. I told her she did not have to take all of her belongings with her. When she insisted, I knew why.

Her mother and I had a chance to meet her dorm mother. She was a nice elderly lady who seemed to be patient with the girls. I knew she would become my daughter's primary caretaker. I hoped Victoria would allow the woman to parent her in some way. I knew she was done with me.

The next few times we saw Victoria again were at her college graduation and again at her wedding. On both occasions we mixed into the crowd like all the other guests. While I was proud of my daughter's accomplishments, I was but a fly on the wall. I was a stranger on the outside looking into the life of my own daughter. My feelings were a mixture of joy and pain.

Over the years we have seen Victoria and her husband William at family weddings and funerals. While we always offered our home, Victoria always insisted on getting a hotel room.

When she came home this week, she was so surprised to see all the changes her mother and I had made over the years to the old house. We took walls down in some areas and put new walls up in other areas. We have new carpet, new paint, and new furniture. We have done a complete overhaul on the old house. She could not see it right away, but over the years we have also done a complete overhaul on our marriage too.

All of my sons still live in Cincinnati and each of them visited several times that week with their wives and children. It was amazing that Victoria knew each of the ten grandchildren just from letters the youngest son has sent her over the years. I see the grandbabies all the time and I confuse their names a lot. I chalk it up to old age.

Victoria, my wife, and I went to visit the youngest son in the penitentiary. Since I have retired I see him weekly and he calls at least once a week too. For his mother and me it has become routine to drive an hour and a half out of the city each Friday morning to visit our son. We walk through a metal detector, submit to a pat search, and make our way through several metal locking doors to see our son. For Victoria I could tell the experience was difficult. I tried to give her a few pointers to make it easy on her. I instructed her to put her picture id in her pocket and leave her purse locked in the trunk of the car, so she would not have to go about the business of having it searched. She followed in step with her mother in locking their purses in the trunk. I assured her I had plenty of quarters in my pocket for sodas for the vending machines for all of us. Victoria looked shocked and amazed that her mother and I were so familiar with the routine, but she also looked relieved at the same time.

When we arrived at the visiting room we were a few minutes late.

It took longer than usual to get through the visiting line today. There was some obvious problem with one of the visitors. We stood quietly as drug sniffing dogs and a line of correctional officers in uniforms handled the problem at the front of the line. A lady was finally escorted out of the line and we entered the visiting room. My youngest son was already there. Victoria and her brother hugged and cried for a long time. It was so good to see the two of them back together again. The two were thick as thieves growing up. We stayed at the visit for the maximum time allowed. We talked, held hands, cried, and prayed together the entire time. Our ride home was quiet and sobering.

Before Victoria left that week, I sat her down with her mother. I told Victoria I had confessed my many mistakes to my wife over the years. I told her we went to counseling with our Pastor for four years to put our marriage and our lives back together. I shared with my wife many years ago just what happened that awful night in Dayton when our youngest son was arrested. I was there in Dayton that day. I saw Victoria leaving the mall that awful night so many years ago. She was crying and upset. I was there. I was there with another woman. Victoria saw me with my mistress and my other baby.

Chapter 23

Victoria

"It was really hard being home in Cincinnati, but at the same time it felt so wonderful. I'd never talked to my parents so much in all of my life as I did in the past week. It was great. We talked about everything. We talked about our past mistakes. We all cried and we apologized to each other for the pain and hurt we caused one another. I feel like such a fool, William. It has taken me to the age of thirty-five to realize I have been harboring so many confusing feelings inside me. I blamed my parents for so many of the negative feelings inside me when in reality they never meant to hurt me. All they ever wanted was the best for me."

"Sweetheart that's all any parent wants for their child."

"William, the bottom line is I ran away from home to avoid the hurt feelings inside of me that I was too immature to talk about."

"Honey, don't be too hard on yourself. You were only seventeen years old. You were just a kid."

"William, it's been eighteen years. It took me eighteen years to gain the courage to be able to return home and face my fears. I was still too afraid once I got there to talk about the baby, my father's other child. Thank goodness he brought up the subject."

"Now everything is out in the open and you all can talk about things now. Did he share with you anything about your younger sibling?"

"Yes. I have a younger brother, Brandon. Daddy ended the relationship with Brandon's mother after I saw him that night in Dayton. Daddy said he could not continue hurting his family any longer. He continued to support Brandon financially. It took him a year to gain the courage to tell mother about the affair and Brandon. It took Daddy and Mother four years of counseling with their Pastor to put their marriage back together. One of the final steps in the counseling included Daddy reestablishing a relationship with Brandon. The Pastor insisted family reunification was essential. Luckily, Brandon's mother was receptive to the idea and Daddy and Mother began to visit with Brandon and became an important part of his life. Now Brandon is away at college."

"Wow. That's an amazing story. Your parents were both strong enough to do the right thing for their marriage and for Brandon. I see where you get your strength from."

"Oh William. My strength comes from a long line of strong people in my family—my grandparents, aunts, and uncles. Remember it wasn't easy for me growing up in a house with five brothers."

"Don't you mean four brothers and a sister?" William chuckles trying to make light of the situation.

"William that's not funny," I stand firm. "My baby brother does not consider himself to be a woman. He does not desire to be a woman. He is a homosexual man and he is very comfortable with his lifestyle."

"You know I was just kidding. I just wanted to see if I could put a smile back on your beautiful face."

"I had a good talk with my mother while I was there too. She told me all about Aunt Gail. Growing up I never knew Aunt Gail could not have children. Aunt Gail always wanted a little girl. So, when I came along Mother thought I was such a blessing; she needed to share me with her baby sister. Mother felt so blessed that she had been able to have six children and felt bad that her youngest sister had not had the same blessing. Besides Mother felt bad for me growing up in a house with five brothers. She thought Aunt Gail could help groom me into a proper young lady instead of the tomboy that I was as a little kid."

"That's sad that your Aunt wanted children, but could not have them. That was wonderful of your mother to share you with her sister. You know, Victoria, I was wondering if what your mother shared with you regarding your Aunt's infertility has changed your mind about starting a family."

"William, I have to be honest. My mother asked me the same question."

"Well, how did you answer your mother?"

"My Aunt's infertility has made me question my decision not to have children. I don't want to end up ten years from now regretting my decision and by that time, I may no longer be able to produce children."

"I need to call your mother and thank her for getting you this far. At least you're not completely ruling out having children. In one discussion your mother has been able to persuade you more than I have during our entire marriage."

"You know my mother is more special than I ever knew. She is so insightful. I never recognized that before. I guess because it had been so long since I spent any time with her."

"Well, you've become pretty insightful yourself."

"Thank you sweetheart. I love you." I lean over and give William a gentle kiss on the lips. We both smile.

"I'm especially grateful to Mother for spending a little time with me in the kitchen while I was home. She taught me how to cook a few of her specialty dishes. So now I'll be able to prepare a few more meals at home."

"Without burning up the kitchen or sending us to the hospital?"

I jab William in the ribs with my index finger and he bends over and laughs hysterically. He tries to get away from me, but I chase him around the island in the kitchen. He circles the kitchen twice before I catch him. I wrap my arms around William's waist.

"You know I have to make a decision about the CEO position at JDL soon."

"No you don't. Take your time sweetheart. I don't want you to rush into making a decision about the CEO position. Our financial situation is strained, but we can get through it. We have some investments that can carry us for a while. So you just take your time and don't worry about the money. I have it all under control for now. I mean 'we' have it all under control."

"Oh William, that's why I love you so much. You're a wonderful husband. You always seem to know just what I need. I'll take my time making the decision, but I'll need you to talk to me about it as I work my way through my decision-making process."

"No problem. I'll always be here for you sweetheart."

Despite all of the talking William and I have done lately. I still have not been able to talk to him about Malcolm. I am not sure if I ever will.

Chapter 24

Joe/C& J Private Investigation Firm

*W*e were making really good progress on the JDL case until the subject of our investigation disappeared for three weeks. It is a good thing I am in so close with Maxine Rogers and I was able to get the inside scoop. Jackson went home to visit her family in Ohio for a week and then stayed home another two weeks to rest up for the CEO position she will assume at the first of the year. When she returns we have little time remaining to break this case and hand over the goods to David Tray. We have narrowed our investigation to three significant points:

First, while Jackson was away we received a report on Jackson from our Cincinnati connection. It appears Jackson's father had an illegitimate child during his marriage. We will hand this information over to David Tray in our full report.

Second, the case report on Jackson's brother's charge of Receiving Stolen Property and Theft were particularly interesting. Every eyewitness interviewed at the shopping mall where the offender committed his crime described a young black female with him. During the trial the defendant *refused to reveal the identity of his companion and took the rap for the case. Coincidentally the description of the young black female is the exact description of Victoria Jackson. This angle may be difficult to pursue, but my Cincinnati connection will give it his best shot. He has a Correctional Officer at the prison where Jackson's brother is incarcerated on his personal payroll. He intends to use the C.O. to squeeze information out of Jackson's brother.*

Third, the real heart of the investigation centers around Jackson and fellow Senior Executive Malcolm Prince. My partner, Constance thinks there is nothing to the telephone calls and meetings between Jackson and Prince. Constance has not pegged Jackson to be the cheating type. In my opinion men and women can never remain just friends. I am sure Jackson and Prince are up to no good and I intend to expose them. According to all of their telephone records—cell phones, work phones and home phones—the two had been talking non-stop until Jackson took her three-week sabbatical.

I hope this information is resolved soon;, last week, Maxine Rogers told me she was falling in love with me. I hope this investigation is over soon; I feel like this time, I have gotten in too deep.

DECEMBER

Chapter 25

Baby Brother

"Peaches, where you been man? I been looking for you everywhere for the last two days?" asked Harold. Harold is a friend of mine, if you can have a friend in prison. Harold is gay, like most of my associates. He might talk a little too much and definitely flares his hands too much when he talks. He is stereotypically gay, as far as I am concerned.

"I've been in the infirmary with the flu all week," I reply.

We are standing in the chow line in the middle of the Springfield Correctional Facility dining hall. There are at least two hundred men sitting at the crowded tables or standing in line waiting to be served. Tonight ham and beans with cornbread on the side is on the menu.

Harold steps in close to me and stretches his neck upward when he speaks, because I am at least two feet taller than him. "I gotta talk to you man," he whispers. "Some weird shit is going on."

I am not immediately alarmed. Harold is more than a little bit paranoid and he just might be off his medication again. He develops huge conspiracy theories when he is off his meds. Still, I am always willing to listen to Harold, even though he is a little off his rocker. I try to console Harold by maneuvering behind him in the chow line. "Ok man, no problem," I say.

We move through the line and pick up the food trays in the cafeteria-style serving line and tote the lukewarm food piled high. We move with the flow of traffic to a table near the back of the dining hall. There is not as much commotion in the back. Harold and I sit side-by-side at the picnic-style table.

"Hey man. You won't believe what's been going down," Harold leans over and whispers. Harold is still stretching his neck upward.

I am willing to listen to Harold, but I am in no mood to wait while Harold stalls and builds his story up larger than it actually is. Harold does that a lot when he is off his meds. "What is it Harold? What's going on that has you so worried?"

"Man, its Officer Snitch. He's been poking around here asking about you and your sister. I thought at first that he musta saw her in the visiting room and he wanted to try to hook up with her, but that ain't it man."

"Well, what is it about my sister Officer Snitch wants to know, Harold?"

"He wanted to know if you talk to her on the telephone or if you write her any letters. Now ain't that some shit. He's getting all up in yo bizness, ain't he?"

"Did Officer Snitch ask you about my sister?"

"No. I overheard him asking Jo-Jo."

Jo-Jo is my ex-lover. We split up on very bad terms a couple of months ago after a five-year relationship. Jo-Jo has been out to get me ever since. I do not know for the life of me why Officer Snitch would be interested in my sister.

"What did Jo-Jo tell Officer Snitch?"

"He told him you keep a whole box full of old letters from your sister locked up in your personals box over in the warehouse."

"I don't know what's going on, but this is strange. Thanks for looking out man." I really am grateful to Harold for telling me this information.

"Watch yo back, man, watch yo back."

Harold sits greedily eating every morsel of food on his tray. I just lost my appetite so I slide my chunk of cornbread over to Harold. He greedily eats up the cornbread.

****

It cost me fifty bucks to get the officer on duty that night to let me into the warehouse to retrieve my sisters' letters from my personal property box. Officer Snitch was asking around about my sister's letters and I would do anything to keep them away from him. Officer Snitch is bad news.

I spent hours that night ripping Victoria's letters into tiny pieces of confetti and flushing them down the toilet. I knew deep down inside the devil was knocking at my sister's front door. I could not be there to protect her as badly as I wanted to be there for her. I stayed on my knees all night. I prayed the Lord would protect my sister and answer her front door.

Chapter 26

Victoria

I return to work, but I still have yet to decide on the CEO position. I am talking that decision out with my therapist once a week. I figure if counseling worked for my parents, it can certainly work for me. Dr. Smith, Ph.D. and I are making tremendous progress with my panic attacks. In fact, I have not had another panic attack since I began therapy. Mentally, I am feeling better than I have felt in a very long time.

I take advantage of the slowed pace at work to tie up a few loose ends. I work closely with a few of the other Senior Executives to complete a few deals. I am careful to avoid Malcolm Prince because I have not yet decided how to put him down gently. I also avoid David Tray like the plague. He still seems to be watching my every move.

This Friday is the company's annual holiday celebration. For the first time in a long time I am especially eager for the holiday season. This year will be very special. William and I are planning to have a traditional Christmas dinner at our house. We have invited both of our families. We are even going to cook the dinner ourselves. I look forward to the celebration and spending time with family. The therapy must really be working, because Mother Jackson, will be staying for an entire week and I am looking forward to her arrival.

****

I arrive at the hotel Friday night for the holiday celebration dressed to kill. I pull off my full-length fur coat and reveal a fitting black off the shoulder evening gown. My silver shoes and purse add just the amount of sparkle needed for such a holiday celebration. My hair is styled in cascading curls and my makeup is flawless. Unfortunately, I have no escort. William is at a celebration for the firm, so I am flying solo once again.

There are at least a few hundred people in the beautifully decorated ballroom. The decorating committee really outdid themselves this year. The place looks like a winter wonderland. There are large red satin bows on each of the chairs, green ivy and white lights are hanging on every wall. Every table is covered with a white linen tablecloth with a gold candle enclosed by more green ivy. There are a few dozen couples on the dance floor trying their best to dance to the music being played by the live band. Most of the others are sitting at tables. But when I enter the ballroom, all eyes are on me.

I immediately begin shaking hands with numerous employees, clients, and their spouses. Both the men and women comment on how lovely I look tonight. I agree with them all. I know I am looking good tonight. I feel good too. I feel like I have been reborn. I feel more relaxed tonight than I have been in years. If William were by my side tonight, the evening would be absolutely perfect.

I cruise the room looking for Max and Joe. I promised Max I would sit with the two of them during the formal dinner portion of the event. Before I know it I feel a tap on my shoulder. I sure hope it is Max. I am already tiring of walking around the large ballroom holding a plastic smile on my face. I turn around to find an incredibly looking Malcolm Prince. Malcolm is sporting a black tuxedo tonight and he wears it well. I am flustered. I step back and take a deep breath.

"Good evening, Victoria," Malcolm says undressing me with his sparkling eyes.

"Good evening, Malcolm," I say trying not to smile too wide. "You look absolutely breathtaking tonight."

"Thank you, Malcolm. You look quite handsome yourself."

"Thank you. If I would not being imposing, I would love to have this dance."

Malcolm does not exactly wait for my reply; instead he leads me by the hand toward the dance floor.

"I would love to," I say so as not to turn Malcolm away and embarrass the both of us.

Luckily a medium tempo song is on. I do not have to dance too close to Malcolm. I play it safe and stick to a simple two step dance motion. I am not surprised to find out Malcolm is a wonderful dancer. I am relaxed and grooving to the music. I am pretty caught up in Malcolm's motions when I feel another tap on my shoulder. "Not now," I say to myself. I turn around to find Max grinning at me. She is holding on tightly to Joe as if her life depends on it. They look ridiculous dancing so closely.

"Hi Max. Hi Joe."

"Hi Victoria. Hi Malcolm."

"Victoria I have been looking for you. I have a table for us when they seat for the formal dinner."

"Great. Thanks Max."

Just like clockwork, a series of bells ring and a voice comes over the speakers asking the guests to please be seated for dinner. As the dance floor clears, I thank Malcolm for the dance. He quickly asks me to have a drink with him later and I agree. I follow Max and Joe to a table in the center of the ballroom. As we are seated I greet the other guests at the table. There is Edward Jones from the seventh floor and his wife. There is Diane Richards from the fifteenth floor and her partner. The rumor mill has it Diane is interested in taking my Senior Executive position if I become CEO. I am sure she purposely positioned herself at my table tonight. Also at the table is an empty chair—a chair my husband should be occupying.

Immediately waiters in black pants and crisp white shirts come out with large silver trays of salad. Without any warning, a young black woman comes and asks to sit in the open seat. I invite her to join us. She introduces herself as Constance Mallory, an intern with JDL on the tenth floor in the Premier Accounts division, Malcolm's division. As the waiters serve the guests, Max begins talking non-stop. I am not listening to Max, I still have my mind back on the dance floor hypnotized by the way Malcolm swerved his hips.

I daydream my way through dinner and I sip on a glass of wine. Once dessert is served, people begin to move about the room freely again. I take the opportunity to head to the restroom in the lobby. As I exit the ladies' room, I am caught off guard by David Tray. Before I know it he is in my face with his ugly wife and a few of his supporters by his side. Just as the heat gets incredibly hot, Malcolm comes out of no where and rescues me.

"Victoria I've been looking for you everywhere. The Mayor is inside and he would like a photo with you before he leaves."

I look at David Tray and his entourage. "Pardon me. I don't want to keep the Mayor waiting."

I watch as Tray and his crew look on with envy. Malcolm extends his arm. I take it and the two of us strut inside the ballroom.

"Thanks for the rescue," I say to Malcolm

"Hey I'll do whatever it takes to get you alone for that drink you promised to have with me."

I smile and relax as Malcolm leads me to a table in the ballroom. We sit and have a couple of drinks and we talk for a long time. Malcolm's chair seems to be getting closer and closer to mine. Finally I realize he is rubbing my leg under the table. I put down my glass of wine and tell him I better get back to mingling. Before I know what is happening, Malcolm slides a room key in my hand.

"I would love to continue this conversation," Malcolm says.

I look down at the room key in my hand. "Malcolm I'm not sure about this."

"I just want to talk. I just want to continue our conversation in private. Victoria, you and I are friends. There is no harm in us talking."

I get up and walk away from the table. The room key is still in my hand and I slide it into my purse.

I meet Max back at her table.

"Joe had to leave. He received an emergency page from his job." Max is still grinning from ear to ear although her man had to leave. Max has two drinks sitting in front of her.

"That's too bad Max. You guys looked like you were having a really good time together."

"We were. We always have a good time together. But, this

gives the two of us a little girl time together tonight." She hands one of the drinks sitting on the table in front of her.

"Come on girl, let's work the room."

Max and I are off and running. We get up from the table and work the room. We are meeting and greeting guests for the next forty-five minutes. Max points out several outfits that are not working for their owners tonight. We have a great time joking and laughing at the outfits, the people on the dance floor with no rhythm and all the drunken partygoers. We have a wonderful time together. Max is absolutely great to have around. I am so glad I can truly call her a friend.

At last we are both exhausted. Our feet are killing us. We sit down and take a break in the lobby for a few minutes.

An out of breath Max says, "I'm going to call it a night. I'm exhausted and my bed is calling my name. This was a wonderful party this year. I really had a great time."

I see Malcom sitting on the other side of the lobby. He stares at me from across the room. "Have a good night Max. I'll be right behind you after I make another trip to the ladies' room."

"Do you want me to wait for you?"

"No Max, you go ahead. I don't want to hold you up."

Instead after Max leaves I head to the elevator. I look back to make sure Malcolm is watching me. He is. I head up to the seventh floor to room 712.

Chapter 27

Constance/C & J Private Investigation Firm

I *have learned you have to be bold if you are going to be a successful*
private investigator, especially if you are a female. I mean Joe is
bold, sleeping around with an unsuspecting woman just for the ben-
efit of the case, but I am just as bold. After walking right up to the table
where Jackson was sitting tonight, I spent the entire dinner getting
nowhere at all in the investigation. So, I decided to keep an eye on Mal-
colm Prince instead. As my luck would have it, I saw Prince make a
transaction at the reservation desk. He took out a credit card, handed it
to the hotel clerk and received two room keys in return.

As quickly as he walked away, I then walked right up to the night
clerk at the upscale hotel and laid down two crisp one hundred bills. I
asked the clerk which room Prince reserved. She wrote the room number
down on an envelope and placed inside a magnetic strip card key as if I
had reserved a room like any other guest. She slid it to me with one hand
as she slid the money into her pocket with the other hand. It never ceases
to amaze me what people will do for money.

I text message Joe to meet me in the parking lot of the hotel. We pass each other just like we are strangers in the night. The untrained eye would never be able to see that when I passed him I slipped the envelope with the room number and card key in his jacket pocket. Joe and I think so much alike. He knew just what to do next.

Chapter 28

Victoria

I exit the elevator on the seventh floor. My heart is beating fast, my hands are shaking, and my palms are sweating. I am definitely nervous. I have never done anything like this since I have been married. I stumble over my feet as I maneuver through the long hallway and I know it is because I have had too much to drink. I have trouble with the card key, but after the third attempt I realize I am trying to enter the wrong room. I am at room number 710. I slide over to the next door and I finally manage to open the door to room number 712.

Once inside I walk through the sitting room and into the bedroom. I sit on the edge of the king size bed and I look around. The room is gorgeous. It looks like a honeymoon suite right off of a movie set. The scene is clearly romantic. I was not expecting this and it really takes me for a loop. I stand up and look inside the bathroom. It is just as gorgeous as the sitting room and bedroom. I turn around and walk back through the bedroom and return to the sitting room. I take a seat on the loveseat. I know I am feeling the buzz of the wine I consumed tonight, because the room begins to feel like it is spinning.

I ask myself over and over again what am I doing here. I have a husband on the other side of town. I still love him. I believe he still loves me too. We just need time together. Time to get back to our love. Time for us. This just does not feel right. Waiting in a hotel room for another man, a man that is not my husband does not feel right at all. I cannot imagine I will feel any better when Malcolm arrives. Then what is the point? Why am I here? I have to get out of here.

I jump up from the side of the loveseat and place the room key on the table. Despite the spinning feeling, I run out of the hotel room. I run away from the elevator, in fear I will run into Malcolm and have to explain my decision. I do not even give my fur coat a second thought. For all I care, the coat check girl can have it. I spot the back stairs and I run all the way down them. My high heels make it difficult, but I never slow my pace. I fly like a bat out of hell until I reach the exit at the back of the hotel. I keep running until I find my car in the parking lot.

****

Malcolm enters the hotel room. He is puzzled. He walks through the sitting room, and then into the bedroom and finally he enters the bathroom. "Where is Victoria?" he asks himself out loud. He sits on the edge of the king size bed for several minutes. He picks up the remote control and clicks on the television. "Oh well," Malcolm says out loud. "The room is paid for so I might as well make good use of it."

Malcolm picks up his cell phone and dials a number in the programmed phone book. It is a number he is all so familiar with. It is done. His booty call is one of the guests downstairs so he knows it will only take a few minutes for his lover to arrive. Malcolm takes a quick shower and covers himself in a towel. His lover enters the hotel room and the two begin to kiss and caress one another familiarly. Malcolm knows a good standby is important. He always has a good lover or two on the side. Tonight's lover is one of his best.

****

Joe nonchalantly walks down the hotel hallway until he reaches room 712. He places a device up to the door and listens inside. Clearly there is heavy breathing going on. Joe concludes Malcolm and Victoria are inside getting busy. "This is my photo opportunity," Joe says to himself. He knows David Tray will pay big bucks for these pictures. Joe slides the magnetic strip key into the lock and the green light appears. The two hundred bucks Constance paid the hotel clerk was well worth it.

He quietly opens the door and slides into the dimly lit sitting room. He quickly sees the two bodies intertwined on the bed in the bedroom, but his eyes have not yet adjusted to the dark room. Joe lifts his camera, careful to get a good angle. He needs to get a full face and body shot of Victoria and Malcolm doing the do. He knows once he begins to click the camera and the flash starts going off the two will quickly separate and grab at the sheets to cover themselves. As he struggles for the correct camera position, the two humping bodies continue to move and the groaning and moaning sounds get louder.

Joe starts to click and the camera flashes frantically. One of the bodies has reached the point of ecstasy and there is a delay response in their reaction to the flashing light. Finally, Joe is able to see clearly now. He gets a perfect shot of Malcolm in motion with a man! After Joe blinks his eyes and snaps back to reality he realizes he has stumbled across a scene very different than what he expected.

The once intertwined bodies separate and are screaming and shouting at Joe.

"What the hell is going on?"

"Stop! Get out of here!"

Joe continues to click away until the entire roll of film is used. He knows David Tray may not be interested in the pictures, but he is certain he can find a buyer who will pay handsomely for the photos. One of the celebrity rags will be happy to have photos of the ex-pro football player in a compromising position. The shouts at Joe continue.

"Get out of here you freak!"

"Call the police! Dial 911!"

Joe makes a fast exit out of the hotel room. He quickly walks down the hall and enters the back stairwell. He rushes down the stairs stopping on the landing of each floor to puke his guts out.

Chapter 29

Victoria

I sat in my car for an hour outside of that hotel. I was frantic and in tears when I ran out of that hotel room. What was I thinking? No other man is as important as the love I have shared with my husband. I was not prepared that night to throw it all away. I love William too much for that.

All of it was my fault. I had no business starting up anything with Malcolm Prince in the first place. He was never really interested in me. He did not want to be my friend. He just wanted to get me in bed all along. I was such a fool. How could I?

The tears poured out of me like a heavy running faucet for a long time sitting there. I cried from the bottom of my soul. That part of my soul I had just allowed so much baggage to spill out of. That part of my soul that is just a scared little girl. That part of my soul that yearns to be protected and shielded from the cruel parts of the cold world we live in. That part of my soul that since opened will not allow me to close it. The hurt and disappointment from deep inside me rocked my body. I felt the motion from my body rock the car.

I stayed in this position for a long time. There I sat, a single car *in the middle of hundreds of other cars, in one of thousands of parking lots in Indianapolis. I sat there shaking, cold and alone. It started to rain. The rain was pounding on the hood of the shiny red car. The rain made it feel colder than the already thirty degrees. The windows fogged. I continued to cry. I was a fool. All of the people inside never noticed I was gone.*

The tears finally dried up. I wiped away the smeared make up from my face and started the car. I starred at the hotel full of happy partygoers as I drove off. A few leftover tears found their way to the surface and fell down my face. I took a deep breath and drove slowly away. Away from all of the people at JDL, away from the foolishness and madness I thought was so important to me. Away from the system that kept my mind racing so fast I was in overdrive. Away from that part of my life I had allowed to consume me—mind, body and spirit. Away from the games people play. Away from the dog eat dog world that just took a bite out of my ass. I sped off towards home. Toward William, the man I love.

When I arrived home, William was not there. I imagined him still at his company party all dressed up in his tuxedo still having a good time. I imagined him standing around holding a glass of champagne chatting politely with some high-profile client or one of the senior law partners. I can just see my handsome husband telling one of many jokes he is so famous for. I imagined him laughing with his professional laugh. Not the laugh he laughs at home when it is just the two of us. He has a talent for making people laugh. People just enjoy being around William. I know I do.

I moved slowly to the shower. I took my time getting undressed and getting under the warm running water. I washed my hair and scrubbed my skin. I scrubbed away all signs of the slimy Malcolm Prince. I scrubbed every part of me that that man touched. I scrubbed my hands, the inside of my right thigh, and my right shoulder.

I was so engrossed in my thoughts, I was startled when I turned around and found William had entered the bathroom. He was already undressing. As I peeked my head out of the shower to greet him, he met me with a kiss.

I made love to my husband that night and together we made a baby.

Chapter 30

Maxine

"The year ended at JDL with a bang! Actually it ended with several bangs! Malcolm Prince showed up on the front page of the local celebrity rag naked and in the bed with another man. I'll tell you everybody was shocked. I mean we all new Malcolm was a ho, but we didn't know he was a homo. His rich white wife showed up at JDL and practically drove her Mercedes through the window of the front lobby she was in such a rush to get to Malcolm. She stepped out of that Mercedes in her bathrobe and hair curlers. She was waving a copy of the celebrity rag and yelling out obscenities all the way up to the tenth floor. When the crazy woman got her hands on Malcolm she hit him over the head with that magazine over and over again. All the women in his office jumped up on chairs and started shouting, "Kick his ass! Kick his ass!" It was like a scene from the Jerry Springer Show. Malcolm was so embarrassed he couldn't get out of the building fast enough."

"And that's not the half of it. David Tray managed to get himself fired. His secretary Dora went into the office to get his agenda for his meeting. She went around the other side of his desk to find it and she happened to look up at his computer screen. David had been in his office getting his freak on. There was an Internet porn pop up on his computer screen. Dora ran out of the office and retrieved the Director of IT. While David was in his meeting, IT was in his office searching through his computer. Come to find out David had been looking at live internet porn 99% of his time at work. No wonder his department was going to hell in a hand basket. When David got out of his meeting, security was standing outside the door with his personal crap in boxes and escorted him straight off the property."

"And if you think that's something let me tell you about Bernard Rich. Everybody knew Bernard had been screwing his young secretary. Come to find out she was pregnant with his baby. Bernard probably was popping Viagra like they were breath mints. Anyway, they ended up eloping to Mexico and Bernard took all of his money with him. He left his ugly wife and three ugly kids here broke."

"This place has been crazy. That's why I'm so glad I'm up here on the twentieth floor so I don't have to be bothered with all the drama going on around here."

"Beep." The intercom sounds on the telephone on Maxine's desk.

"Yes may I help you?"

"Max can you come in? I'm ready to go over my schedule for the week."

"Yes, Ma'am," Max replies.

Max leans over her desk and continues her discussion with the mail clerk. "Speaking of being pregnant, you ain't heard it from me, but our new CEO will be wearing maternity clothes soon enough. Now let me get myself in there before she blows a gasket."

Max rushes into the CEO's office with her Pocket PC in hand, ready to take notes and schedule meetings for her boss.

"Max, please call Ms. Vaughn with the Sisters Helping Sisters Program to schedule Tuesday to discuss setting up the mentoring program. Schedule Mr. Williams with Martin College Wednesday to discuss increasing the number of interns we have on board at JDL from the historically black college. Also schedule Rev. Derricks from Mt. Prospect Church for Friday to discuss JDL supporting the food bank and temporary housing provided by the church."

"Don't you think you're moving awfully fast? You've only been in office for two weeks and already you've scheduled to meet with the half of the city. I promised William I would take care of you and not let you overwork yourself before the baby comes."

"Max, I'm just making up for lost time. I've sat idle for much too long. It's time for me to make a difference. Remember I told you if you accepted the position, we would be very busy. I'm committed to making a positive change."

"I don't mind the hard work. I'm so proud of you and I'm proud to be by your side."

"Well then, let's get to work. There's no time to waste."

I stand up to exit the room. My mind is fixed on rushing to my desk to schedule the number of meetings for my boss. I am almost at the door, when I hear one last command.

"Max, one more thing please."

"Yes, Ma'am?"

"I want to thank you for everything. Thank you for being my friend and being by my side through it all. I never could've made it without you."

I smile brighter than I have in a very long time. "Anytime, Ms. Jackson. You know you're my girl!"

Questions for Book Club Discussion:

1. Why was Victoria on overdrive ?
2. Discuss the nature of Victoria and Monique's friendship.
3. What was Victoria's attraction to Malcolm?
4. What feelings about your childhood did Victoria's experience stir in you?
5. Do you think Victoria told William about the near infidelity with Malcolm? Why or why not?
6. Discuss what the group knows about the phenomenon of black men on the "Down Low".
7. Discuss the additional challenges Black females face in Corporate America.

9 781598 581539